A WOLF for a SPELL

by
Karah Sutton

illustrated by
Pauliina Hannuniemi

ALFRED A. KNOPF
New York

For Mom. The story starts with you.

THIS IS A BORZOI BOOK PUBLISHED BY ALFRED A. KNOPF

Text copyright © 2020 by Karah Sutton
Jacket art and interior illustrations copyright © 2020 by Pauliina Hannuniemi

Visit us on the Web! rhcbooks.com
Educators and librarians, for a variety of teaching tools,
visit us at RHTeachersLibrarians.com

Library of Congress Cataloging-in-Publication Data is available upon request.
ISBN 978-0-593-12165-8 (trade) — ISBN 978-0-593-12166-5 (lib. bdg.) —
ISBN 978-0-593-12167-2 (ebook)

The illustrations in this book were drawn in Photoshop and textured with handmade watercolor patterns.
Book design by Bob Bianchini

Printed in the United States of America
September 2020
10 9 8 7 6 5 4 3 2 1
First Edition

CHAPTER 1

Fear sank its jaws into Zima as she recognized the smell of magic. She pressed her nose to the ground and sniffed again. Like moonlight and decay—it burrowed into her nose, slippery and sinister. She shook her head and huffed to clear out her nostrils.

A shiver rippled through Zima's silvery-gray fur. She knew what the smell meant.

The witch was nearby.

It almost seemed like the witch was following them. This was the third time Zima had smelled magic in the past three days.

Her little brother Potok sneezed and scratched his paw at his snout. Together Zima and Potok backed away, out of the cloud of scent and behind a clump of spiky evergreen trees.

But Leto, Potok's littermate, kept his nose to the ground. He turned to Zima with his ears back and his black fur on end. *We should get Grom,* he said.

It was the right thing for him to say. Grom was their older brother and the leader of the pack. He would know what to do about a witch.

But why did they need Grom? Zima was the second oldest. Surely Leto could trust her to handle the witch without Grom's help.

Potok let out a whimper and pawed at the dirt. He clearly wanted to get away from the smell as much as she did.

She tried to take on an air of authority as she voiced her disagreement. *We will be safer going to the home place,* she said, referring to the glen they'd marked as their territory, where they'd sleep for the next few days. *We go the way we came—to the river—and follow it back.*

It would take much longer to go that way, of course, but it would give them a wide berth around the witch. And it would keep them clear of the dangers of the forest—towering hogweed plants that could kill a wolf with a single touch, unexpected shafts leading to caves that could trap a wolf for days, poison streams that gurgled with Waters of Death. Navigating the forest was dangerous business.

She waited for Leto to give the signal that he would follow her lead.

But he didn't.

His body language spoke clearer than words: *I want to call for Grom.*

He wanted Grom to lead them. Zima stared Leto down, trying to shake away the hurt that clung to her chest. But instead, he raised his nose to the air. With his jaw jutting forward, he prepared to howl.

Before he could, a rustle ahead made Zima's ears prick.

She nudged Leto and pointed with her snout. He swallowed the howl. Together they turned to peer at something beyond the grove where they stood.

A figure was just visible, lurking between the trees.

The witch?

But there was no smell of magic about this person.

Zima crept closer and crouched behind a large rock, with Leto following close behind. His tail began to wag as he caught the scent Zima tasted on the breeze. Potok's nervous breathing pulsed in the clearing behind them, where he kept his distance from the danger.

It was no witch. The thing, moving through the woods mere whiskers away, was a human girl.

The human hummed to herself as she picked her way along an unseen path, clutching a worn piece of fabric about her shoulders. The woven coverings on her feet rustled with

each step. Zima searched for the glint of a knife. No weapon was visible, but she must have one hidden somewhere.

Zima fought the urge to flee. This was her chance to prove that she could take care of her brothers.

A conversation with Grom from a few months before swam in her memory. He had pressed a heavy paw on a length of twine. One end of the twine was wrapped around a sapling, and the other was tied around the neck of a fox. The fox's struggles must have tightened the cord until he collapsed and breathed no more. Zima couldn't unsee the fear still frozen in the fox's eyes, or the long scratch marks he had left in the dirt.

They are getting bolder, Grom had said. And it was true. The humans were setting more traps deeper into the forest, and the shift had been sudden and swift, like a new wind carrying great black clouds. The question was, how many more of them were coming, and how much longer would it be before one of Zima's pack got hurt?

Grom had read Zima's thoughts in the hang of her tail and the twitch of her ears, and he nodded. *Something has changed,* he said. *The danger grows by the day.* A fierce need to protect the pack burned in his eyes as he said, *From now on, we must take no chances. If you see humans, kill them, before they kill you.*

Zima shuddered. She knew what Grom would tell her to do.

What she had to do.

She had to kill the human.

Her eyes focused back on Leto. He hadn't moved. *We need Grom,* he said again. He began to retreat from her, his back paws brushing aside soil-colored leaves.

No! said Zima under her breath. *The human will hear you. I can do this, alone.* She repeated the thought to herself. She could do this. She could *do* this.

But the tilt of Leto's ears showed his disbelief. He didn't trust her to protect him.

She had to prove him wrong. She crept closer to the human and closed her eyes, focusing on the scents of hair and sweat, and smoke from kitchen fires. She knew the smells from the only time she'd ever been to the village, when her father had taken her, before he died, at the peak of the warm season.

Her father used to say that humans and wolves could coexist if they left each other alone. But Grom had taken a harsher approach since he became the new leader of the pack: humans were deadly and an increasing threat to life in the forest. *Kill them, before they kill you.*

It is too dangerous, Zima, said Potok, his green eyes aglow between the branches of his hiding place. *Wait for Grom.*

He didn't think she could do this either.

They were both wrong.

With her eyes closed, Zima sniffed the air, feeling the

exact place where the human stood. She mapped out the precise height and distance she would have to leap to take the human by surprise. Leto would be impressed. He had to be.

When she opened her eyes again, she glanced toward Leto to make sure he saw, but he was gone. Potok too. They'd left Zima alone with the human.

Zima dragged her claws through the dirt in disappointment. Leto was going to call for Grom. Soon she would hear a howl and . . .

. . . and the human would too.

Zima looked up. If she waited much longer, the chance to surprise the human would be gone. Now was her moment to attack, to prove that she could protect the pack just as well as Grom.

With narrowed eyes, Zima slunk around the rock and behind a wide oak to get a better view of the human. If she could get the girl by the neck, she could snap her jaws and the human would be dead in an instant.

Zima moved right behind the human and crouched to spring.

The human reached up to tug on the fabric covering her shoulders. Then she stopped, her hand hovering near her neck.

Zima recognized the stiffness of her posture and the twitch in her hands. It was the look of prey that knows it's being watched.

The human called out some words in her language. Her voice quivered, bouncing through the darkness like a bird searching for its lost chick.

There was nothing to do but attack the human, noiselessly. It was now or never.

But then the human made a sound. A whimper.

The girl was frightened. But humans didn't feel fear—they always attacked first.

Kill them, before they kill you. Grom's words rang in her ears and threaded through her thoughts, roots buried inside her and holding on tight.

Zima set her jaw. She had to do this to protect her family. Keeping them safe was as vital as the blood that thrummed in her throat. She readied her legs to leap.

A howl pierced the air. Leto, calling for Grom, giving Zima's location.

The girl whipped around at the sound. Her eyes grew wide as they caught sight of Zima with her bared fangs and taut tail.

Their eyes locked for a moment.

Kill them, before they kill you.

The girl blinked. She took a step back. And another. She glanced behind her at the path.

This girl wasn't preparing to attack, she was preparing to flee.

That wasn't right. Humans were dangerous, but this human wasn't trying to fight.

When Grom had uttered the words, Zima had imagined herself staring down the shaft of an arrow, bravely leaping to attack a hunter before he could release the string. Killing a human that had no weapons, made no move to attack . . . surely this wasn't what Grom meant?

A thought flickered in Zima's mind, burning bright before she had a chance to snuff it out: she didn't have to kill the girl. She could leave, and the girl wouldn't follow.

Zima closed her mouth and straightened her ears. Finally, she scrambled away, back around the boulder.

The girl's quick breaths formed a panicked rhythm.

Suddenly shame washed over Zima. What was she doing? She'd given herself away, failed to kill the girl, and was now hiding like some sort of twitchy little rabbit. And Leto and Grom would arrive at any moment.

There was still time to do it. She peeked around the boulder. The girl met her eyes.

And then the girl smiled. Not a sinister, cruel smile. It was alight with kindness. She lifted a little hand and waved it.

Zima ducked behind the rock. She couldn't bring herself to do it, not now that she'd looked in the girl's eyes and seen no hint of the threat that Grom had assured her she'd find.

Keeping motionless, she listened for the girl's breathing. After some minutes there was a rustle of movement, and soft footsteps pattered away from the clearing.

For what seemed like an age, Zima sat there, too afraid to move. What had she done? She'd put compassion for a human above the safety of her pack. She'd let a human wander free in the middle of the forest. Her mind raced, her stomach heavy with embarrassment and shame. It took her a moment to notice that a new smell had seeped into the clearing.

It was the stink of magic, of the witch she'd detected just before. It filled her nose and throat, making her gag.

Her chest tightened. She had to get away from this place.

CHAPTER 2

T he witch Baba Yaga peered through the trees, watching the young wolf. Of all the wolves she'd seen, this was the first to step away from an attack. She could see the

conflict in the bristle of the wolf's fur. The tension straining the muscles of her legs. The wolf wanted to do something, to attack the little human girl, but she chose not to.

That was exactly what Baba Yaga needed. The gray wolf . . . a wolf who wouldn't put up a fight.

CHAPTER 3

Nadya crept away from the clearing, her mind buzzing like a swarm of bees. She'd met *another* wolf, been close enough to smell the pine needles clinging to its silvery fur. The thought sent a shiver of excitement down to her toes. And in that moment the wolf had backed away from *her*.

The others were wrong. She *could* navigate the forest on her own. Ignoring the nervous trembling still dancing along her fingers, she reached into the little bag tucked into the folds of her skirts and tugged out a crumpled sheet of paper. Dirt-colored lines were scratched across its surface— a smudge to indicate a familiar cluster of trees, a squiggle to signify a stream. Laying the paper on the ground, she licked a finger and pressed it into the dirt. Carefully she used the tip to draw a little wolf with pointed ears and a bushy tail. Wolves moved around, she knew that, but it was helpful to know where she'd spotted one.

There was still a lot missing, but every day she ventured farther into the forest, every day added a little more to it. It didn't matter what the others said about the dangers of the forest—*she* knew how to navigate them. And when the day came when she finally left the orphanage, no one would follow her. They'd be too scared to enter the forest themselves to chase her down.

She sat, adding the new features she'd spotted that day to her map, taking care to mark poisonous plants and places where the earth fell away into craggy chasms—sudden holes in the ground that would trick an unwary traveler.

Her lips pressed into a hard smile.

No one knew the forest like she did.

She was so close to being ready. She could feel it. Soon she could leave the village for good.

When the light grew too dim to continue, she stood and brushed herself off. Katerina would be sure to notice the dirt smudges on her dress—nothing escaped those large eyes. Oh well, soon Katerina would be off to the castle in the north, living her new perfect life as the perfect bride of the tsar, and Nadya would be on her own in the forest, making her way to the great road that led south to the city and a new life.

The paper fluttered as she held it up, trying to snatch enough slivers of fading sunlight to see where she was. Was she near the sheer rock face? No. The dried-out stream? No again.

She made her way down a slope, placing each foot in its woven bark shoes carefully so as not to slide on the loose rocks. Her foot twisted as she neared the bottom and she lost her balance, her arms flailing before managing to snatch hold of a tree's branch. Her heart jumped. She had nearly fallen into one of the great openings in the ground. Little pebbles slipped out from under her feet and tumbled into the crevice, clinking against its stone walls.

Her hands burned. She released the branch and stumbled away, examining her palms. Deep red marks crossed her hands. They stung, but she didn't have time to worry. She checked her map again. Had she seen this crevice before? It was hard to tell in the dim light.

Her pulse was pounding louder in her ears, trying to drown out the frogs and crickets that were beginning their nightly chorus.

That boulder crouching like a huddled giant, had she seen that before? Nadya stepped toward it. But as she approached, she discovered that these trees were unfamiliar too. They crowded around her, strangers looming.

No, they weren't strangers. She knew this forest. No one

else in the village could find their way through it like she could, and no one else dared to.

But the frogs croaked the truth.

Lost. Lost. Lost. Lost.

Somehow Nadya was lost in the woods.

human towered over her, seven in all, watching her like stone spirits. The smell surrounded her, thicker than fog. A crack and a snap split the air. And then the witch was before her.

Baba Yaga.

Zima had never seen her, but there was no mistaking the cane in her bony hand and the smell of magic clinging to her like smoke. Her skin was as rough and wrinkled as the bark of a pine, and what little gray hair she had stuck out all directions from her head like many twigs forming a crown. Stone-gray teeth punctured shriveled gums.

Go away! barked Zima. *Keep away from me!* She panted,

CHAPTER 4

The smell of the witch had begun to surround Zima, thick as fog, making her body stiff with alarm.

The witch was closer than she had ever been. Zim needed to get away, but she couldn't tell which way to The scent was everywhere, clouding her senses. She co detect a safe path.

She stumbled away from the rock, slippin' leaves and bumping into trees. Every hair on stuck out straight as a pine needle. Her legs w right—they dragged along the ground as t' with rocks. She pushed herself upright, b

Before her was a clearing she'd nev of a small hill. Rock structures twice struggling to force each breath through her tightened throat. But as she prepared her front paws to run, the witch made a gesture. Roots sprang up from the ground, ensnaring Zima's legs. The more she pulled at them, the tighter they wound around her.

"Silence, pup," the witch said calmly. "I take as little pleasure in speaking to you as you do to me."

The witch could speak the language of wolves.

But Zima's amazement was short-lived, and she answered with a growl.

I am not falling for your tricks.

The distrust between the wolves and the witch went back hundreds of wolf generations. No wolf ever interacted with the witch without walking away changed. At least with a human you could search for a knife or an arrow. But the witch's magic was hidden, and could be used for any number of devious purposes. *You are worse than a human,* Zima said through bared teeth.

The witch let out a thunderclap of laughter. "Oh ho, am I? The humans setting traps, chopping down trees, lighting fire to your home? You say I am worse?"

Baba Yaga glided closer to Zima, her footsteps silent, her skirts dragging across the ground. "It is the humans that worry me," she said, tracing a gnarled finger along the top of her cane. "I came here because I have a task to give you."

A spiteful retort froze in Zima's throat. She coughed and spluttered in surprise.

Baba Yaga took advantage of Zima's silence to continue. "I am the guardian of this forest. You would be serving not just me, but the forest itself, through your delivery of what I need."

She seemed to have no doubt that Zima would say yes. Certainty twinkled in her eyes. But the witch was trying to trick her, of course she was.

I do not believe you. I know you have been following us, I have smelled you. Zima stared at the witch, taking in the wrinkles of her lips, the purple flecks in her eyes. The realization hit her. The humans in the forest, the witch tracking her pack—they were linked. *You are working with them.*

Baba Yaga let out an amused cough. "Stop talking nonsense!" She jabbed her cane at the ground. "How can I side with them, when they pose as much danger to me as they do to you?"

Zima had to fight to ignore the witch's words. She tried to wrench her paws away from the ground. But the roots held fast. She lost her balance and tumbled forward, her snout slamming into the dirt. Still, her paws didn't move.

I do not care what you want. I will not help you, said Zima, her growls muffled against the ground.

The witch's lips hardened into a thin line. "Fine, then. But it is not only *I* who you betray with your refusal." Her mouth curled into a smile, revealing those gray teeth, jagged as knives.

Baba Yaga struck her cane into the ground. To Zima's surprise and wonder, a giant stone bowl floated toward them from just beyond the crest of the hill. Baba Yaga climbed inside the bowl and seated herself, her knobbly knees jutting out on either side. "Come to me when you change your mind," she said. The stone bowl took flight, skimming along the ground and carrying her out of sight.

Zima's legs trembled, but she forced herself to stand. The witch's words clung to her bones like moss on stone. There was something evil in them.

The witch had a plan. And Zima had narrowly escaped being part of it.

CHAPTER 5

adya swallowed. Steady breaths . . . she just needed to find something familiar. Something she had marked on her map that would help her find her way home.

Tears stung her eyes, but she fought to hold them in. How was she supposed to run away through the forest if she couldn't even find a path to her own village? She stamped her foot. She would find her way back, just to prove that she could. And if she couldn't, the orphanage wasn't a home to her anyway, so what did it matter if she never returned?

"Lost, little one?" a voice boomed.

Nadya whipped around. Before her was a man on horseback, his shadow sharp in the light of the newly risen moon. A fur cloak clung to his arms and shoulders like ivy.

As her eyes adjusted, it took Nadya a moment to tell where the fur of the man's cloak ended and his pointed black beard began. At last, she recognized the angular features of Tsar Aleksander. His dark eyes glittered in the shadows, heavy black brows arching above them.

No, no, anyone but him. Nadya's stomach churned as she imagined the smug look of satisfaction that would drape itself across Katerina's perfect face when Nadya was returned to the orphanage by the tsar himself.

She turned away. She could pretend she hadn't seen or heard him.

The golden bridle on his horse jangled, sending musical tones ringing through the grove.

"I asked, 'Are you lost?'" said Tsar Aleksander. His deep voice was warm; his tone had a hint of amusement.

She gritted her teeth and turned around, remembering at the last minute to give a formal bow, her hand on her heart. His eyes fell on the hem of her skirt, and she remembered the dirt smudges.

A desire gripped her to pretend she had nothing to be ashamed of, not the state of her clothes or getting lost in the woods. With a lift of her chin, she raised her eyes to meet his. "Just making my way to the village, your illustrious highness," she said.

"I thought as much," he said, and the starlight danced across his cheeks and the bridge of his sharp nose. "My dear

Katerina sent me to look after you." He shook the reins, and his horse trotted forward, closing the distance between them. "She knew you would be in the forest somewhere, despite her advice never to enter this dangerous place."

Nadya sighed. *Of course* Katerina would send someone to look for her. "Katerina worries more about the forest than I do," said Nadya, hoping it made her sound brave.

The tsar chuckled. "In that, Katerina and I are the same. It is why I have planned the great hunt for the day after our wedding." His black horse shifted its balance, as though the tsar's words made it uneasy. "The forest must be tamed."

She had already heard him brag before about the hunt, in one of his visits to Katerina since the announcement of their upcoming wedding. "The greatest hunt anyone has ever seen," he'd called it, then vowed, "I will burn back the forest that has crept ever closer to the castle these many years." Nadya clenched and unclenched her jaw. She didn't like the sound of it at all, but she also knew the tsar would never change his mind just because she disliked it.

Tsar Aleksander extended a hand toward her from his towering position in his saddle. His black sleeves shimmered with gold-threaded embroidery. "Come, little one," he said, "I'll take you home."

Nadya winced at "little one," but said nothing.

He swung her up behind him in the hard leather saddle, the fur of his cloak cushioning her against his back. She wrinkled her nose. The tsar thought that hunting animals made him a conqueror of the forest. But he didn't know the forest like she did. Even if she had gotten lost just this one time.

Together they rode back, the tsar following some invisible path. Nadya tried to remember the turns they took, and each unusual rock or tree they passed, so she could add them to her map. At last, the trees thinned and the village opened out before them, a series of crooked wooden houses fighting to stand upright among a lumpy chain of hills.

The orphanage stood closest to the edge of the forest, no welcoming warmth drifting from the stone oven in the kitchen at the back, no laughter or music flowing through the cracks in the wooden walls. Only thin blankets and stringy stew that could barely fill a hungry belly. For a moment Nadya enjoyed the warmth that came from riding behind the tsar. Katerina was going somewhere she'd never be cold or hungry, or so tired after a day's chores that she nearly fell asleep while trudging up the stairs to bed.

After the tsar had helped her down from the horse, Nadya turned to bow at him as he dismounted. There was a rustle of skirts and a soft footstep that could only mean one thing. "Nadya, you know better than to go wandering off into the forest by yourself. If Baba Yaga found you for her dinner, you would have no one to blame but yourself. . . ."

Nadya turned to face Katerina, quick to hide her injured hands in the folds of her skirts.

In the soft moonlight Katerina seemed even more beautiful than usual. Though her blue sarafan and headdress were as plain as the clothes of all the orphans, Katerina's were cleaner and crisper than Nadya's. Somehow Katerina always managed to avoid getting any dirt on her at all. It was no wonder the tsar had chosen her to become his tsaritsa—it was a fairy-tale story of the orphan girl from the woods becoming royalty that would be told by firelight for years. The tsar held to an old forest tradition that anyone who gave him a gift that he deemed worthy would be honored with a royal favor. When he visited the village, Katerina offered him one of her beautifully woven cloaks, soft as a feather and more intricate than a spider's web. In return he named her to be his bride.

Katerina knelt so that her eyes were level with Nadya's. The smooth expression broke with a crease across her forehead as her large eyes bored into Nadya's. "Who will look after you when I go away?" she said, and Nadya couldn't miss the hint of true concern that weighed down her words. "Mrs. Orlova can't watch after you like I do." She glanced at their mistress, watching them with a frown from the doorway. The old woman didn't dare to snap at Nadya in the tsar's presence.

Ignoring the warmth of Katerina's hands on her arms, Nadya said, "I'll be fine. I don't need anyone." But that was a lie. She didn't want to be alone; it was just her only option.

The soft, searching look in Katerina's eyes continued for another moment before she stood and said, "And, dear, what have you done to get your dress so filthy?"

There it was. Perfect Katerina once more.

Nadya looked away toward the forest, dark tree branches beckoning her with long twig fingers.

From the shadows, a single glowing eye stared back at her.

CHAPTER 6

Baba Yaga wove through the trees in her stone bowl like a leaf carried on a stream. Behind her she dragged branches to sweep away the track left by the drifting and dragging of her stone mortar and pestle through the dirt. The ancient bowl didn't navigate as smoothly as it once did, and she had to keep her legs tucked in so they wouldn't knock into the trees.

It was no wonder she avoided leaving her hut any more than she could help it.

A bear paused in tearing at brambles to watch her fly past. His paws flexed and she urged the mortar to fly faster. She had no time for him.

The mortar gave a shudder, as though asking her which way to turn.

The witch lifted her nose into the air, sniffing. The smell of magic had always guided her, the delicious scent of earth and moonlight forming a path through the forest. But her nose could not find the smell. She sniffed again, searching for the flowers and feathers that floated on the breeze. For the blood of humans, the most pungent scent of all.

Nothing.

She would have to find her way through memory alone. Her thin fingers were sharp as they rubbed her eyes and nose while the mortar continued to fly. She was getting old. Her senses weren't what they used to be. Her eyes were simply tired, but her nose—it seemed to have lost its use entirely.

Come to think of it, she couldn't remember the last time she'd smelled death, or even anything at all.

CHAPTER 7

The thunder of Grom's heavy paws signaled his approach. Relief lit his face as he saw Zima, but it was quickly replaced by a frown. *What happened?* his voice thundered at Zima. *Where is the human?*

Leto arrived, just in time to hear Grom's question. He stood close behind their brother, his sides expanding with deep breaths after his run, waiting for Zima's answer.

Zima bowed her head. She couldn't bring herself to tell them that she'd let the human escape. They'd once been inseparable, she and Grom. But on the longest day of the year a fire had spread, killing both their parents.

Their mother and father had ordered Zima and Grom to get the younger pups away from the danger. They obeyed, carrying Leto and Potok as far as they could, waiting in safety for their parents to follow the scent trails they'd left behind.

Their parents never returned.

After that, Grom stepped up as leader of the pack, and the five moons since had seen more humans in the forest setting traps and tracking their pack. Grom wasn't Zima's friend anymore, he was her guardian. Stern and distant, he moved with an intensity that made Zima's legs quiver. Her heart ached at what she had lost—not just their parents, but her closest companion.

Now, at the thought of admitting she'd spared the human, it felt like she'd made the wrong choice. She'd been too weak to go through with it.

But at least she had refused to help Baba Yaga. That much she could be proud of.

The witch appeared—Baba Yaga, Zima said.

Grom's ears twitched in surprise while the rest of his body grew stiff with alarm. *Baba Yaga, here?* he asked. He glanced around the clearing, as though expecting the witch to emerge from the trees at any moment.

She came to assign me a task, Zima said. Then she couldn't help but feel pleased with herself as she added, *But I refused her.*

She waited for Grom's approval, a sign that she had done well.

Grom's expression was rigid, immovable. He turned to Potok, who had crept close to stand at Zima's flank. *Go. Back to the home place,* he said. Potok flinched but obeyed. Grom then turned to Leto. *And you. I need to speak with Zima alone,* he said. Leto followed Potok from the clearing as though he'd just been given a stern lecture.

Grom stomped to the far side of the clearing. The earth trembled under his muscled frame. *Tell me what happened,* he said, *everything.*

Zima tugged her claws through the dirt. Telling the whole story meant admitting that she'd let the human go. She began with her and her younger brothers tracking their final meal before starting the trek toward the home place. But when it came time to explain how she had hesitated to kill the human, Zima choked. She couldn't face Grom's disappointment. So instead, she slid straight from when she crouched, no farther than a leap from the human, to when she'd detected the smell of magic.

She'd never kept the truth from him before. Ever. It felt like it confirmed all the distance that had grown between them since the fire. Like a canyon, it opened out before her, and soon it would be too far to jump across.

When she got to the part where she accused Baba Yaga of siding with the humans, Grom let out a growl. Zima stopped, her mouth still open, startled into silence.

The witch spoke to you, and instead of running away, you spoke back? Grom said. There was a dangerous rumble in his throat.

I tried to run, but she used her magic to hold me to the ground, Zima said. She demonstrated the way her paws had been ensnared. *I could not move!*

Grom thought on this for a moment. *The witch uses words to distort and confuse, and now it seems she can force you to listen.* He began to pace back and forth across the clearing, moving so swiftly that his paws left barely a trace in the dirt. *What has she done to you? Did she turn you against us?*

No! Zima said. *She said she was in danger from the humans, just like we are.*

Grom froze, and Zima realized immediately that she'd said something horribly wrong. *This is how she tricks you. You should have called me as soon as you smelled the witch, but you did not. And then you failed to kill a human.*

So he knew, without her telling him. Zima pawed at the ground in shame.

You let your fears possess you. You will never protect this pack until you control them. There was something in the curve of Grom's forehead and the stiffness of his shoulders that she had never seen before. Something between anger and heartbreak. He let out a sigh. *And,* he said, *you kept the truth from me.*

I was ashamed, said Zima. *It was wrong—*

Humans lie. The witch lies. Wolves do not lie.

Zima opened her mouth to speak again, but Grom silenced her with a glare more piercing than a hunter's knife. *I wish our parents were here,* he said. *I do not want to punish you. They would know if you . . .* But he stopped, not finishing the thought.

If I what? Zima asked.

Grom shifted, his paws planted firmly on the ground, the way they might when he faced a threat.

And Zima realized. *She* was the threat.

. . . if the witch cursed you, he said.

No! Zima said, shock and hurt rippling through her fur. *I would have known, I would have felt it if she tried to curse me!*

Would you? said Grom. *I cannot take that risk.*

It was a mistake, said Zima, *I know that now. But it was a choice, I made a choice—*

Grom turned away from her, swiping a paw across his ears. *Quiet!* he said, cold and sharp as an icicle. *I need to think. I must decide what to do.* He resumed pacing.

Zima clamped her mouth shut, but she wanted to argue that she had chosen not to kill the human because she'd thought that that was the right thing to do. It had nothing to do with witches or curses. It was Zima, only Zima, trying to make the right decision. Because the forest was becoming more dangerous for their pack than she had ever known. First the humans, now a witch—threats were circling like birds of prey. Zima thought of the fox in the snare. Her pack was no match for the weapons of humans, or the powers of the witch. If she'd killed the human, it might have prompted an all-out attack from the village. At least now they had a chance to decide what to do next.

Their mother had said the forest was so large that a wolf could run for a hundred days and not reach the other side. *We should run,* Zima said.

Grom stopped in his tracks. *You,* Grom said, giving his words the weight of a boulder, *want to run?*

Zima answered with her body language—her tail upright, her ears forward.

Yes.

It was the only way to protect the pack.

And when the humans follow, what do we do then? Grom asked. *Do we keep running?*

His tail flicked. *No,* Grom said. *I have another plan.*

A lump of disappointment rose in Zima's chest. He hadn't even considered her suggestion. But she swallowed, hoping to crush the feeling flat. *What is it?* she asked, trying to sound eager.

Perhaps I will tell you, he said slowly. *But not now.* He turned to her, and there was almost an apology in his eyes. *I need to know that the witch has not altered you, that I can still trust you.*

A human's arrow could not have pierced Zima's heart as deeply as her brother's words. Trust, honesty . . . that was everything to a pack. The canyon had widened so far between them that Zima could never hope to leap across it.

Zima lowered her gaze. She wanted to argue, but heartbreak held her rigid.

Grom's growls still swam through his words as he said, *For now, you are not to go near the others. You are not to venture from the home place. When I have decided I can trust you again, I may reconsider. And—*he paused, preparing to add even more to the weight of dishonor he had heaped upon her—*if I ever find out you have spoken to that witch again, you will be banished from our pack.*

Zima thought she detected a hint of sorrow in his words, but whatever she heard was gone in an instant.

Now, let us return to the others, said Grom. He leapt forward and disappeared into the shadows.

Part of her wanted to stay behind. But instead, she followed close at Grom's tail as he led the way to their home place.

As soon as Zima caught the familiar scent of the home place, Grom signaled for her to keep her distance. For the rest of the night, Zima was left to herself. She couldn't play or hunt, and was forced to sit alone listening to the hooting chorus of nearby owls. Grom had taken Potok and Leto away from the clearing, out of sight and earshot of Zima. Her heart sank lower. Whatever plan he had for protecting the pack from Baba Yaga and the humans, he meant to keep Zima out of it.

Somewhere within her, lightning flashed. This wasn't fair. She'd spent her whole life protecting the pack. When Grom became their leader, she'd followed his every rule, believing that it was for their safety. Backing down now, letting the others work to protect the pack while she sat and watched and did nothing . . . it was unbearable.

She'd start with Potok. He was less headstrong than

Leto, and hated violence. The two were the same size and age but could not be more different. If she could find a moment with him alone, maybe she could get him on her side. He would be overjoyed at the thought of running from the humans.

Finally, the sky began to lighten, and it was time for rest. Zima nestled her chin on her paws. As the others returned to the clearing and everyone drifted off to sleep, her last thought was to will herself awake before anyone else. Potok's certain excitement at hearing her plan sang in her ears, drowning out all sounds of her family's snores.

CHAPTER 8

As Nadya dipped her hands in the cold water of the washbasin, a shadow fell over her. She looked up, expecting Katerina to chide her for the scratches and scrapes she'd earned in the woods, but instead found herself staring at Mrs. Orlova, the mistress of the orphanage. She was not an old woman, but there were hard wrinkles around her eyes and mouth, like canyons that had been worn into rock over time.

"What will I do with you once Katerina is gone, hmm?" she said, though it didn't seem as if she actually expected an answer.

Nadya wanted to respond that Mrs. Orlova wouldn't have to do anything, that she would leave the orphanage for the woods before long, but she kept her lips pressed tight together and instead finished washing her hands. She yelped as the woman reached out and took Nadya's wrist, holding her hand up so that the wet palm glistened in the candlelight. The tree she touched in the forest must have been poisonous, because the red marks had begun to swell and blister.

Mrs. Orlova frowned. "I only want to find each of you girls nice families. But I can't help you if you don't want to help yourself. Wandering off into the woods, neglecting your chores and sewing . . . you'll never impress a family by being disobedient," she said, examining the wound. "Katerina knew this. She tried to get you to understand. At least you sometimes listened to *her*." She let Nadya's wrist go, and Nadya pulled her hand close to her chest.

Mrs. Orlova sighed. She patted her dark hair, which was slicked back into a severe bun. "I had hoped it wouldn't come to this," she said, "but Mr. Demidov needs a new servant. It might be time I send you to him."

The pulse in Nadya's wrist quickened. Mr. Demidov lived west of the village, miles away from the forest. Working as a servant was undesirable enough, but if she went to him, escaping into the woods would be almost impossible.

Regret flitted across Mrs. Orlova's expression like a moth. "At least this way, you'll have a future." The expression vanished, and her features were once again in their usual stern arrangement. "I will write him tomorrow."

The woman's quick footsteps were already thumping against the wooden floor toward the door. Mrs. Orlova blew out candles as she passed, hushing the other girls, who were huddled under blankets in their shared beds. Nadya opened her mouth to call after her, but only a croak came out. When the door closed, Nadya was swallowed by darkness.

She could leave. It was sooner than she'd planned, but it was an opportunity. If she waited, how long would it be until Mrs. Orlova sent her to Mr. Demidov and cut off her access to the forest completely? She crept toward where her cloak hung on a peg, her fingers itching to snatch it so she could leave this very night.

The door creaked open again, making Nadya jump, but the soft footsteps, light as a cat's paws, soothed her with their familiarity.

"Nadya?" said Katerina's voice, and light from her single candle blossomed in the darkness. "Is that you by the basin? I thought you'd be asleep by now." Unlike Nadya, Katerina was allowed to come to bed later, along with the other older girls. But Nadya wasn't ready for sleep, not after Mrs. Orlova's proclamation.

Nadya had known Katerina since she was two years old, when an illness had swept through Nadya's old village and claimed her family. Katerina had been at the orphanage since she was a baby, abandoned by no one knew who. All the girls looked up to Katerina as almost a big sister or a teacher. In those first few years, when Nadya cried to soothe the ache of missing her parents, only Katerina's songs could stop the tears.

Katerina moved to sit on Nadya's bed, and motioned for Nadya to settle beside her. She'd brought some herbs and medicines with her, and she spread them out on her lap. With gentle but assured swiftness, she took Nadya's hand and examined the cuts across her palms. Katerina dabbed a salve over the blisters, holding tight to each wrist so that she could work even as Nadya flinched from the burn. Nadya hated it when Katerina babied her like this, but the salve did soothe. And wounds dressed by Katerina always seemed to heal faster than when Nadya took care of them herself. At

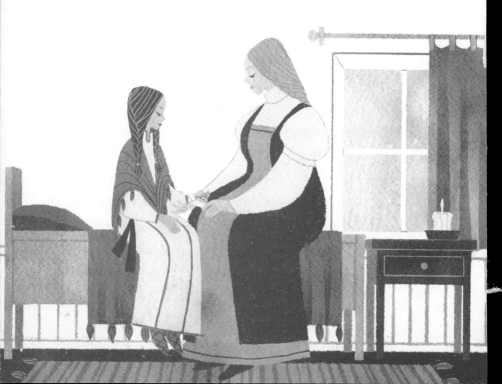

last, Katerina wrapped Nadya's hands in soft bandages and let her go.

She gave a sigh. "I was so embarrassed, Nadya, at the tsar having to rescue you today."

"He didn't rescue me!" Nadya snapped, even though that wasn't quite true. Katerina's words stung, but not as much as the tears that pricked at the corners of Nadya's eyes.

Katerina sighed. "I'm sorry, that was unkind," she said. "I only . . ." She paused, and there was a rustling of fabric as she smoothed her skirts. "I used to wander into the forest too. You probably don't remember—you were still a baby, but when I was younger than you are now, a family wanted me."

It surprised Nadya to see a tear slide down Katerina's cheek. Had she ever cried before? "I gave them a gift," she continued, "a flower I'd found in the forest. I didn't know it was poisonous. It should have killed me to touch it." She glared out the window, an angry crease between her brows. "I lost my best chance at a home, but from then on I knew to stay out of the forest. And you should too, Nadya. It curses everything it touches."

Nadya squeezed her fists, her fingers pressing into the bandages. She didn't have a chance for a loving family like Katerina did. Families found Nadya reckless, disobedient, useless, just like Mrs. Orlova did. If perfect Katerina couldn't find a family to love her, what hope did Nadya have?

No, her only hope was to escape into the forest, and every minute that Katerina sat talking to her was a minute that Nadya wasn't preparing herself for the journey. She pinched her eyes closed.

But Katerina hadn't finished. "Mrs. Orlova wants to send you away. So I've asked"—she paused, and Nadya felt a hand take hold of her shoulder—"I've asked Tsar Aleksander if you can come to the castle with us."

Something warm filled Nadya's insides, like soup trickling down her throat to fill her stomach. She? Join Katerina and Tsar Aleksander at the castle?

Katerina's next words shattered her thoughts. "But he doesn't like that you go into the forest alone. So he has agreed that you can come to us on the wedding day if Mrs. Orlova says you have behaved as you should from now until then."

The warmth that had briefly filled Nadya turned ice cold. Not go into the forest? Behave as she should? Convincing Mrs. Orlova that she deserved to go and live in the castle would be impossible.

Even if she did manage to convince the tsar, could she continue to behave that way in a new life at the castle? She would be expected more than ever to always know what to do, how to act, what to say. She would feel the eyes of many more people on her whenever she had dirt smudges on her nose or wrinkles in her dress.

She started to shake her head, but Katerina squeezed her shoulder. "Just think on it, please?" said Katerina softly. "It would be a comfort to have you with me."

It was a feeling Nadya couldn't remember ever having before: feeling *wanted*. Katerina's fondness, with all its scoldings and criticisms, flowed deeply enough to invite Nadya to join her at the castle. And if she didn't go, what then? Would that fondness snap like a dry twig? Would she lose the closest thing she'd ever had to family?

Those feelings, that *wanting*, was a string knotted around Nadya's waist. And as Katerina went to bed and the slow music of her soft breaths finally filled the room, that string tied Nadya to the orphanage for one more night.

CHAPTER 9

A pointed roof peeked through the trees as Baba Yaga neared her hut. Her memory had not faltered—she could still remember the way, even if her senses had worn a little with age.

She lifted her hands into the air, palms facing the hut. Like the eyes of a creature asleep, the hut's windows were dim, and smoke drifted from the chimney in faint snoring breaths.

"Little hut," she said, calling to it as a friend, "turn your back to the forest, and your front to me!"

The hut stirred. It shifted, jostling dry leaves from the branches brushing against its walls. Sleepily it turned, steps lowering from between its dim windows. The door creaked open to welcome her home.

Her hut would help her in her plan. In her centuries of life, everything always seemed clearer from the inside, next to the fire.

She was tired. So tired.

It was tempting to stay inside forever. To forget the dangers that awaited her, to hide from the world and its evils. All she needed was someone to do the work that was expected of her. Who would take up the task so that she could rest?

CHAPTER 10

he other girls in the orphanage buzzed with excitement as they went about their chores. They seemed to swirl and swarm around Katerina, leaving Nadya in what should have been peaceful solitude. For the first time, no one was paying any attention to her. On any other day she would have been delighted at the change, enjoying the silence and the lack of anyone telling her what to do, but today it left her alone with too many thoughts.

If she stayed at the orphanage, behaved as perfectly as Katerina always had, then there was a chance that on the morning of the wedding in a week's time she would have a new home at the castle. If she didn't manage to impress Mrs. Orlova, then she'd go back to her old plan to escape into the forest. She could live in the woods, or travel beyond to the city. Either way, she'd be free to do things as she pleased and not as others demanded.

Grain danced in the pails that she carried to the chicken coop behind the orphanage. The handles pressed against her bandaged palms, but she managed to deliver the grain without dropping a single kernel. That was a first step toward proving that she deserved to join Katerina at the castle.

The cheers and bustle of villagers could already be heard along the road that wound behind her. From what she'd been told, the road skirted the edge of the forest, all the way north to the castle a few hours' walk away.

Sunlight gilding the birch leaves made the forest appear inviting, despite the poisonous plants and fearsome animals within. But going to the castle would certainly be safer than the forest. She would never want for clothes or warmth or a bellyful of honeyed pancakes and gingerbread from the castle kitchens. . . .

Maybe she could be as graceful, as polite, as faultless as Katerina. And the castle could feel like a home, with Katerina and Tsar Aleksander like her family.

Movement caught her eye, and she turned to find a lump of brown fur leaping toward her. She laughed as her wolf pranced in friendly greeting, his one eye bright and his tail wagging like a puppy's. His other eye was sealed shut by a jagged pink scar that ran from his ear to his snout. This was her wolf, the wolf who had long visited her to play and beg for treats. He was the first to show her that she need not fear the forest.

"You've come just in time!" she said to him. She ducked into the chicken coop and reemerged with a couple of eggs, which she tossed to him. He caught them in his mouth and crunched heartily.

"Nadya! What are you doing?" The voice broke through her cheered daze like a rooster's crow. Her insides tensed, and without thinking, she shooed her wolf away. He watched her in confusion for a moment, lifting and setting down his paws as though uncertain of what to do, but when Nadya glanced behind her at Katerina's fast approach, he seemed to understand. In a flash he disappeared into the safety of the trees.

"Was that . . . a wolf?" said Katerina as she came to stand at Nadya's side.

"No," Nadya lied quickly, hoping Katerina hadn't gotten a good look.

But she had, of course she had, and the crease between her brows appeared.

"You can't lie to me," she said. "The tsar will never allow you to join us if he knows that you lie." In celebration of her journey to the castle, Katerina was dressed in what must have been a gift from the tsar. Silver threads glinted in the sunlight and the fine sapphire blue fabric flowed like a stream. The clothes suited her, as though she belonged in them. They would never look so well on Nadya.

Katerina moved to stand in front of Nadya, blocking her view of the trees. "That was very dangerous," she said gently. "That wolf is not your pet."

The hope of joining Katerina at the castle battled with her fears of never entering the forest again and—at the same time—not being good enough to be accepted. She had to try. If she ever wanted a home and family, she needed to do what Katerina asked.

"I will try harder," Nadya said. "I will make you proud."

"I know you will," said Katerina, pressing a palm to Nadya's cheek. Then she reached into her small travel bag and withdrew a carved wooden doll, its grass hair wild and untamed. The crooked smile on its face looked as if it had been painted on by Katerina herself when she was very small.

"I've had this doll all my life," said Katerina. "Will you keep her safe for me?"

Nadya let Katerina place the doll in her hands, but grumbled, "I'm too old for a doll."

Katerina smiled. "You're the brave one. I need you to keep her safe."

No one had ever given Nadya anything before. It would have been a lot easier to say goodbye if Katerina had left with a scold or reprimand instead of a gift. Nadya mumbled what she hoped sounded like a thank-you and pulled the doll close to her chest as Katerina's soft footsteps padded away.

But from the road Katerina turned and said, "Make sure to put on your warm wool. You can't run around without it just because I'm not here to remind you. I expect snow soon."

Nadya narrowed her eyes. That was the Katerina she knew. Before she could think of a response, Katerina had disappeared around the front of the orphanage.

Voices cheered and cried in the distance. Katerina and the tsar must have been saying their final goodbyes to the other orphan girls.

Nadya looked behind her, hoping that she might find her wolf staring out at her from the edge of the forest. But he was nowhere to be seen. If she succeeded in joining Katerina in the castle, she would lose him, and no one would understand the heartache that would cause.

She stood alone, picking at the bandages on her hands. The fabric had begun to unravel a little, and she tugged the strip off to examine her wounds. The skin was smooth without a hint of redness. As she bent and flexed her fingers, she could still feel where the wounds had been, as though the forest had marked her, but no sign of the cuts remained. Katerina's salve had worked wonders.

CHAPTER 11

A twig snap jolted Zima awake. The midday sun peeked through roving clouds overhead. All around was the scuffle of boar and barks of roe deer who, unlike wolves, preferred daylight as their waking hours.

Zima lifted her head, wondering what could have made the noise that woke her. Grom and Potok were each sleeping peacefully, their tongues lolling from their mouths. It took her a moment to realize that Leto was gone.

She rose and slumped to the edge of the clearing where the pack slept. But Leto was nowhere to be seen.

Leaves crunched beneath her carefully placed paws. The forest floor glowed amber in the sun as she trotted along, following Leto's scent.

She wove her way past poisonous nightshade berries and mushrooms, the scent guiding a safe passage into a part of the forest she'd never entered before. Zima shivered, though the chill air was calm. After tracking the scent over two hills and beyond a stream, she still hadn't caught up with him.

She picked up speed, stretching her muscles, bounding over roots and rocks. Soon Zima lost track of where in the forest she was, knowing only Leto's scent and using it to guide her further.

The smell of fire crept through the air, and her heart slammed against her chest. But it wasn't the stench of sky-high flames scorching trees in the forest, just the small, smoky fires of human wood-burning ovens.

The realization snapped at her with sharp-toothed jaws. Leto was heading toward the village.

No, he couldn't be. He knew better than to put himself in such danger.

Zima broke into a full run, the messy, flailing run of a wolf with fear nipping at her tail and gnawing on her heart.

She stumbled over a tree stump. There seemed to be stumps everywhere. And just in the distance, riding the wind, came the sound of human chatter. Low voices like the patter of rain mixed with high-pitched laughter.

Zima! What brings you this way? came a call from among the trees, making her jump.

With a glance behind her Zima recognized Veter, the lone wolf. He bounced as he trotted toward her.

Zima tried to keep running but her paw ached from her stumble. She shook it and walked on, shouting over her shoulder, *No talking now, Veter—I must find Leto!*

But Veter bounded in front of her to block her path, his brown tail wagging.

You can stop to play, he said. *I am so happy to see you.* His one eye was round and bright.

Zima winced. She couldn't see him without thinking of the fire; the same fire that killed her parents had also killed his entire pack. Ever since then, Veter had lived near the village, stealing whatever scraps of food he could find and sleeping behind wood piles.

She carried on down the path, but the lone wolf bounded about, inviting her to play.

Zima ducked past him and picked up speed. Veter panted as he galloped to match her pace. *Where does Leto's scent lead?* he asked.

The village, she answered. The word caught in her mouth, dry, like she'd swallowed a bunch of dead leaves.

I can help you! He hopped on yet another tree stump. *I know the village. I know how to get around there without getting caught.* His tongue hung from his mouth as he panted joyfully. *We can have fun searching!*

Zima stopped in her tracks. She dug her claws into the ground. "Fun" was the last thing she'd call this. Veter didn't understand the danger, that her heart pounded like a stampede. It was hard to focus on the scent when she had to answer his questions.

It is not fun. It is dangerous. She arched her back, indicating she wanted to be left alone. *Leave me.*

Veter's ears flattened. He shrank down like a shriveled berry.

Zima sniffed and raced away from him as fast as she could manage. For a moment there was a surge of guilt from her stomach to her throat. When there was no sound of paws hitting the ground behind her, she was half-glad he had listened to her, and half-angry with herself that finding Leto now fell solely on her.

She lost Leto among all the other smells of the village. Horses, chickens, pigs, all scratching around in their hay-filled pens. Smoky fires and oil from lamps that had been put out when the sun rose. Soap and clean clothes. Even the distinctive smell of freshly splintered wood. All of them recognizable from the only other time that Zima had been close enough to the village to smell them with her father.

Zima had gotten angry at him for taking them so close to so much food, and not allowing them to have any. She didn't know that in only a few moons he would be gone.

Wolves and humans have a long-held pact: If we stay out of the village, they will stay out of the forest. It has always been this way, he'd said. *No matter how hungry you are, no matter what you seek, you must never enter the village.*

But he was wrong. The pact was broken. Humans had started entering the forest. And now Leto was going into the village.

Before her, the road was packed with men, women, and children. So many people. Did the humans always gather like this? The children chased each other with sticks, laughing and yelping, the tree-bark coverings on their feet heavy with mud. Women pulled fabric tight around their heads to protect themselves from the frigid air, their cheeks and lips rosy as they giggled. Many of the men wore fur on their heads, making them look like strange forest creatures. The humans all had their heads turned in the same direction, as though watching and waiting for something to happen.

She sifted through the many smells, trying to find the one she knew to be Leto. At last, she caught it. He was nearby. He must have just passed this way.

Carefully Zima crept along the edge of the woods. This was different from his usual smell. Sweet, like ripe berries. It was bursting with the scent of his feelings, and he reeked with excitement.

And then he appeared. Just a few bounds away from her, half-hidden by the trees. He trotted behind a cluster of villagers. They had their backs to him, but he was close to them, too close. A human with a bow and arrow could easily shoot him, could even throw a knife where he stood. But none of the villagers seemed to notice the young wolf behind them, weaving close and then away, poking his nose about. He was searching for something.

CHAPTER 12

A sharp sound—almost like the trumpet of a goose—pierced the air, three blasts. Excitement rippled through the crowd of villagers. They shivered, like something had rubbed their fur the wrong way and they were shaking themselves to set it right.

Zima crouched, aiming to grab Leto by the scruff of his neck so she could drag him away from the humans into the safety of some nearby brambles. Silent as the wind, she sprang.

Leto turned his head as Zima flew through the air toward him. They collided and she knocked him to the ground, pinning him under her. Rolling away from the humans, they tumbled down a small hill and just out of sight.

Zima, what are you doing here? Leto hissed when they stopped rolling. *Grom told you to stay at the home place.*

The pity in his eyes stung more than if he'd slashed at her with his claws.

Zima growled softly, low enough so the villagers wouldn't hear. *Why are you here?*

I am not to tell you, Leto said.

Was this part of Grom's plan? Zima didn't move, keeping the much smaller Leto pinned under her. That same trumpeting sounded again in the distance, and the people exploded with chatter.

The two wolves needed to get out of there. They were dangerously exposed, and who knew when the humans would let their attention stray from whatever was going on. Every passing instant there was the risk of a human turning around and spotting them within reach of their arrows.

She pulled her paws away from Leto, letting him stand, then shoving him backward into a jumble of ferns and berry bushes.

Now hidden from the villagers' view, Zima whirled on Leto in a panic. *Father told us never to enter the village. What about the pact?*

Leto bristled. *Humans have been invading the forest. The pact is finished.*

Zima couldn't believe what she was hearing. *So Grom sent you here into this swarm of villagers?*

We did not expect so many.

Then we must go. You can come back here when they have gone.

Leto stood, poking his nose between the fronds to peer out again. *No, I need to watch them. I want all the humans to be here—it means I can report to Grom.*

Report what? Tell me what is going on!

The growl in Zima's throat startled Leto. He turned to her, no trace of fear in his eyes, only surprise. Had she been Grom, he would have answered her question immediately. After a long moment, he sighed. *Weapons. We plan to take human weapons. Arrows, traps, everything.*

So this was Grom's scheme. It would lessen the threat of humans for a while, but at what risk? Leto would get hurt before they got anywhere close to the completion of this plan.

But before she could protest, the villagers began to cheer. Zima jumped, ready to dash deeper into the woods, but Leto stayed put. He kept his head poked through the brambles, watching.

Zima pressed forward, taking in the scene. Leto's eyes were focused on the villagers closest to them, with weapons strapped to their backs. There were quivers full of arrows. Men held roughly hewn bows in one hand. Past them, the reason for all the commotion emerged. It was a wooden box

perched on wheels, pulled by a team of horses. But while the other carts in the village were of rough, splintery wood, piled high with goods to take to nearby villages, this one was enormous and elaborate. Sunlight bounced off the polished wooden beams of its roof. Below, windows were covered with thick heavy cloth, and the doors were framed by intricate carvings of two eagles, their wings outspread.

As the thing passed a gap in the crowd of villagers, Zima saw a graceful hand, so gentle that it might have floated away on the breeze, sweeping aside the fabric in one of the windows.

Then the hand's owner, a young human woman dressed in blue, moved into view. She had a round, moonlike face that glowed with apparent happiness. Her eyes scanned the crowd, taking in each person one by one, until at last the cart rolled around a bend in the road and the woman was lost from view.

Like fog clearing, the villagers turned and began to walk in the opposite direction toward the village. Small children raced ahead and the adults followed behind chattering excitedly at what they'd just seen.

But beside her, Zima could feel the tension in Leto's legs and tail. He'd glimpsed something.

Zima looked back, watching the crowd. There was nothing that she could detect to put Leto on guard.

Then she saw it.

One of the villagers, distracted in conversation, had leaned his bow against a tree behind him. It was too close to him. He would notice if it disappeared, but for the moment, his back was turned.

A flash of dark gray fur whipped past Zima. She tried to call to Leto to stop, but her fear of catching the villagers' attention made her swallow her cry. Instead, she dashed after him, nipping at his tail and missing. He darted up the low slope and extended his neck to snatch the bow in his jaws. But as he turned around to smile in triumph at Zima, something made him pause. Zima followed his gaze, and her breath caught in her throat.

Behind Leto down the road was a villager boy, and his eyes were locked on them.

CHAPTER 13

The chair scraped against the wooden floor of her hut as Baba Yaga pulled it away from the table. She stared at the fire until it burned her eyes. Her plans had begun to unravel. Without a wolf, she would fail, and the tsar would triumph.

The forest had whispered to her that a wolf was the answer, and she had spent days following and approaching different packs. But the wolves hated her, just as they had for hundreds of years. Up until now, she had never found this a concern. She was happy to stay sheltered within her hut and to leave the wolves to themselves. But the forest had once again begun to chant its soft song: *Find the gray wolf, find the gray wolf,* and Baba Yaga couldn't help but wonder why the forest had commanded her to seek the creature least likely to assist her.

How the forest anticipated that a wolf would help, she had no idea. Would the wolf track down the tsar, hunting him as though he were its prey? Or did wolves have their own unique magic, something she had never encountered?

None of that mattered now. Not a single wolf was willing to help her. Not even the young female who had spared that little human girl with the shawl.

The forest was wrong. Baba Yaga had wasted too much time already, trying to convince a wolf to join her, when no wolf was ever going to agree. There was less than one week left until the next full moon.

But there was something else she could do. One last attempt she could make to thwart the tsar. And it was her only option now.

CHAPTER 14

The human boy reached out his little hand and pointed a shaking finger at Zima and Leto. Whispered words to the adult standing next to him were lost in the jumble of rattling carts and the laughing conversations of other humans.

Her legs shaking, Zima crept away from the road with uncertain steps. The ground seemed to tip and tilt beneath her. The bow was still clenched in Leto's mouth as he trailed Zima to duck behind a moss-covered log.

Zima poked her nose out and peered over the log. The man next to the child was now peering toward them, in the direction of the boy's accusing finger. The man's hands were moving toward the bow and quiver strapped to his back.

Kill them before they kill you.

But Zima's courage dropped out of her like a downpour unleashed from a rain cloud. There were too many humans. If they attacked one, more would fight back. She and Leto couldn't possibly defeat all of them. She wanted to call out that she wouldn't hurt them, that she just wanted to go to her home in peace.

But it was no use. They wouldn't understand her.

Run, she said to Leto.

Leto's ears flattened, but he didn't make a move.

RUN!

She turned and hurtled into the forest. Leto followed close behind.

The shouts of human voices pierced the air like the screeches of hawks. There were several voices—the hunter must have called other men from the village to his aid. Their feet thumped behind her and Leto, sloshing in mud and dislodging rocks.

And then an arrow whizzed past her ear. It hit a tree nearby, piercing the tough bark with ease.

She snapped her head back to Leto, but he was fine. The arrow hadn't touched him. He overtook her, leading the way through the trees.

Zima darted one way and then another, hoping it would confuse the humans as she tried to navigate through the forest, always keeping Leto in her sights. She stumbled across a stream and up the slope on the other side. Pebbles dislodged by her paws tumbled down behind her.

Poisonous weeds and toxic springs blocked their path, and they wove through and about, leaping over sudden pitfalls and thundering rapids.

Another arrow pelted the branch of a tree overhead. Zima flinched and forced her legs to run as they'd never had to before.

The voices behind her grew distant. The humans must have lost sight of them.

She kept running.

Only after the human shouts died away completely did Zima slow to a walk. She forced herself to breathe calmly as they ducked between branches to enter a small clearing

encircled by pine trees. The trees stood like humans shoulder to shoulder, forming a wall of branches and needles that shielded the clearing from its surroundings. Leto released the bow from his mouth and collapsed to the ground next to her, panting.

Zima rounded on him in a fury.

What a—dangerous—thoughtless—thing to do! She spit as she spoke, and the words came out in a jumbled mess of angry thoughts.

Leto sneered, baring his teeth. *I did what I had to do! This is how we will keep the pack safe!*

Not if you die first! Zima snapped. *If this is Grom's plan, soon we will not have a pack to protect!*

Leto's ears folded, and a look of shame washed over him. *I was only supposed to tell Grom where to go. He did not instruct me to take the weapons myself,* he said. *But I cannot stand by doing nothing! I need to help!*

His words reminded her of her own anger with Grom. *How can he possibly think our small pack can disarm an entire village of humans?* she asked.

He hopes to gather other packs. We can band together for the safety of all of us, said Leto.

Zima snorted. *That will never happen. The packs have never united, and they will not for a plan as dangerous as this one.*

They will! cried Leto. *You will see! Grom's plan will protect us.*

We have a choice, she said, choosing her words carefully, *to disarm the humans, or to protect the pack.*

Leto's muscles tensed. *What do you mean?*

I think we need to leave. To go somewhere deeper in the forest where the humans cannot find us. It is the only way to protect the pack without anyone getting hurt.

You . . . , Leto said, his eyes narrowed in concentration. *You want to run away?*

But before Zima could answer, a voice, muffled by the pine trees, sounded behind them. *Are you safe?* The voice came as a fearful whine. *I heard humans shouting.*

Zima turned. Veter stepped cautiously into the clearing, his brow furrowed, every whisker tight with concern. She hadn't even heard him approach—the cluster of surrounding trees seemed to block out all sound.

We are safe, Zima said gently. *The humans followed us, but we managed to outrun them.*

Relief lit Veter's face. *The human smells are everywhere. I was worried—something might have . . . but I am glad no harm has come to you.*

Leto let out a low chuckle.

What is so funny? asked Zima.

I am standing between two wolves, said Leto, *one who wants to be friendly with humans, and one who wants to run away from them.*

Zima's tail curled. *You have seen the traps. You heard those arrows. We will not win a fight with them.*

A growl rumbled in Leto's throat, too big and threatening a sound to come from such a small wolf. *You would rather run away than defend our pack from the humans invading this forest.* He bent his forelegs and stared down his muzzle at her, ready to fight. Zima stared into his blue eyes, trying to calm him, to show that she didn't plan to fight back.

That is your weakness, Leto said. *You refuse to fight.*

The sound of thrashing trees made them all turn around.

The young human man, the one who had held the little boy's hand, burst through the wall of branches surrounding them. His jaw was rigid, and his hands clasped a bow with a ready arrow nocked to the string. He didn't leave the protection of the trees, and instead stood nestled between them. But he pointed the arrow directly at Zima, his hands shaking.

Her ears flattened, Zima stared down the long shaft of the arrow. The hairs on her neck stood on end.

Zima fought to think clearly. If she stayed put, the hunter could hurt them all. If she moved first, the hunter would surely kill her, but it might give Leto and Veter time to run away.

She crouched, her eyes fixated on the hunter's throat, but before she could leap, there was a flash of fur as Leto vaulted over her. He roared and snarled as he flew. A howl tried to escape from Zima's throat, but nothing came out. The hunter threw aside his bow, and together man and wolf wrestled, growls and shouts filling the air.

Then Zima saw it. The silver glint as the sun flashed against the hunter's knife.

Without thinking, she lunged toward the hunter. She snapped at the hunter's legs and hands, and at Leto, trying to pull him away from the human.

A yelp pierced the air and Leto went limp. The hunter shoved the young wolf off of him, wiping blood from his face. He stumbled to his feet and bolted away from her through the trees. Zima leapt forward to follow him, but a groan from Leto made her stop. She caught a final glimpse of the hunter as he fled, and then turned to look at her fallen brother.

CHAPTER 15

Leto lay crumpled like a wilted flower. His gasping breaths filled the clearing.

Zima rushed to his side, sniffing, licking away the flecks of blood on his fur. She hoped it had come from the hunter.

And then she saw it. A gash in his side oozed blood, the tangy scent filling her nose. Leto lifted his head and attempted to flop over, then winced, his eyes rolling back. His head hit the ground hard.

She had to get Grom.

But what could Grom do? He could only clean Leto as she could. If Leto stayed like this for long, he would die.

She needed someone who could do more, someone with power. She needed someone with magic.

The grim choice taunted her. Only one person had the power to save Leto: Baba Yaga. And Baba Yaga had come to Zima for assistance. If Zima agreed to perform the witch's task, the witch might heal Leto in return.

But Grom's warning echoed in her ears: *If I ever find out you have spoken to that witch again, you will be banished from our pack.* She would never regain his trust if he knew she'd gone to the witch for help.

None of that mattered now. Leto was bleeding too heavily. If saving him meant losing her place in the pack, then that was what she had to do.

Zima turned to Veter. The lone wolf stood at the edge of the clearing, watching in horror as the blood pooled on the ground. *I know where we have to go,* she said. *Help me carry him.*

As gently as she could, Zima clutched the nape of Leto's neck between her teeth. Fortunately, her brother was still small enough that she could drag him this way without hurting him. Veter's whole body was shaking, but he moved to imitate Zima, grabbing at fur near Leto's leg. Together they heaved back, pulling Leto along the ground.

Grunting with the effort, the two wolves trudged through the forest. It was awkward, and they moved unbearably slowly, but step by step they advanced, toward where Zima had smelled the witch only the day before. Veter followed Zima's lead, not asking where she was taking them or who it was that Zima thought could help. *Nearly there,* Zima whispered to Leto when he whimpered, though their journey had just begun.

When they first caught the scent of magic, Veter gave Zima a hard, questioning look, as though she'd revealed that *she* was a witch. His nose wrinkled, and he let go of Leto. *Where are you taking us?*

Zima avoided his gaze. She didn't answer.

You seek the witch? Veter asked, his jaw trembling. *Zima, have you lost your senses?*

Zima snorted. Maybe she had? Only a few days before, she would never have considered going to a witch for help.

But Veter stopped walking and gave her a look so serious it made her insides squirm.

Zima, listen to me. I cannot go with you to the witch. And you must not go either.

Only she can save Leto, said Zima. *And I will do what I must to keep my brother alive.*

She will change you, Zima, Veter whimpered. *Your pack must know the same stories as mine. Wolves who sought that witch's magic, despite the warnings, and came back altered. Cursed. You cannot trust her—*

Then leave, she cut him off. *Go to Grom. Tell him what happened. But I am going to her.*

With more effort than she thought possible, Zima moved one paw after the other. Step by step, away from Veter, until she was dragging the whole of Leto's weight. She turned her head from Veter, fighting the urge to beg him to come with her, to say that she was too scared to go alone. But after an endless moment he scampered away, back to safety, to tell Grom what she'd done.

One paw and then the next. It was hard to know where she was, but the strong smell of magic told her that she was moving in the right direction.

Zima peered ahead, and saw a looming form. It was a hut, Baba Yaga's hut. It was smaller than she'd imagined, but there was no mistaking it. The hut was raised, balanced on long legs as tall as the trees. Like chicken legs, they were bony and ended in clawed feet.

This was it. One more step and Grom would never forgive her.

Behind her, Leto groaned.

Zima took a deep breath to calm the pounding of her heart and pressed forward.

CHAPTER 16

A tapping at the window made Baba Yaga twitch. It was only the raven, of course, but every time she heard a sound, she felt a stab of dread that a visitor was trying to make their way inside. She slowly pulled herself to her feet and moved to open the window.

The raven hopped over the sill, his sleek feathers glinting purple and turquoise in the firelight. He bowed his head and folded his wings respectfully before lifting his beak to face her again. He blinked, his black eyes unusually grave. *They've gone,* he said.

"What do you mean?"

They left in his carriage. It is headed for the castle.

Baba Yaga stamped her foot, sending a shock up her

bones. She could not allow the tsar to defeat her. She would not.

Wolf or no wolf, she had to end this.

Baba Yaga paced in front of the window, her cane clunking with each step. She knew what she had to do, but she had no idea how she could achieve it, not in the time left until the full moon. She turned to the raven. "I need to find the family."

The raven scratched at the wooden sill with his claws. *But you don't know where they are. I've visited every village around the forest, and I've uncovered no trace of their where-abouts.*

"I *must* find them. They are the only ones hungry enough to take his castle from him."

But how? The forest cannot see them. They are concealed from its magic.

A howl from outside the hut rattled the thin floorboards. There were scratching and scuffling sounds below.

She moved toward the window. Her eyes struggled to bring the figures outside into focus. There were two of them, light- and dark-gray, the smaller one lying motionless on the ground. Then something in the movement of the larger one caught Baba Yaga's eye. It was the female wolf she'd met, the one who had been in the clearing with the little human girl.

The wolf had changed her mind after all.

Baba Yaga retrieved the dagger from its hiding place. All the pieces were coming together, a picture of a plan forming in her mind.

She turned to the raven. "Not sight," she said, smiling. "Smell. I know how I'll find them." She lifted the dagger to admire the gold inlaid along its blade and the blood-red jewels on the bone handle.

"I will smell them."

CHAPTER 17

Zima howled. She dashed around the legs of the hut, looking for an entrance. She yipped and jumped, scratching at the chicken legs with her claws.

A groaning sound from above shook her bones. Zima scampered back, away from the legs. As she looked up, she could see two windows glaring down at her. There was no door.

Zima shuffled her feet and a paw accidentally nudged Leto's side. He gave a moan of pain.

With much creaking and squeaking, the chicken legs slowly bent, lowering the hut to the ground. Steps folded down from between the watching windows like a mouth opening its jaw, revealing the door.

Her eyes were drawn to the entrance. She stood captivated, too afraid to move for a moment, then looked to Leto. His breathing was slow and shallow. She grabbed his scruff with her teeth and tried to drag him closer to the hut. A trail of blood stained the ground behind him.

As she tugged, the door crashed open. The powerful scent of magic seeped from the entrance.

"Were you forced to come here," the witch croaked, "or did you choose to come?" She smirked, and her mouth was as crooked as a winding stream.

I chose . . . but I was forced . . ., Zima struggled to answer. *My brother is hurt, and I need your help. . . .*

"Why should I help you? You refused to help me."

The words froze Zima's heart. The witch had no feeling, no kindness. Veter was right.

I need you to save him, Zima said. *I will give you anything.*

Baba Yaga held up a hand to silence Zima. Her eyes were bright, and that crooked mouth stretched into something that might have been a smile.

Hope tugged at Zima's chest. This was it. The witch was going to save him.

The witch pointed a finger at Leto, lying on the ground, and made a beckoning gesture. Zima started to explain again that Leto couldn't move, but the crone shushed her. Baba Yaga turned around and shambled back into the hut. With a crack and a snap that sliced the silence, grass and vines sprouted from the ground, lifting Leto into the air. In a wave, the grasses carried him along, past Zima and toward the steps. Zima stared. Long vines lifted him up the steps and into the hut.

Without waiting for an invitation, Zima took a deep breath and followed.

The magic odor worsened. It oozed from the walls and clogged the air. Zima's eyes watered; she coughed and blinked to try and clear them. The inside of the hut was cluttered with shelves that bowed under the weight of many containers and jugs and, Zima noticed with alarm, a pile of skulls. Beneath the shelves was the giant stone bowl that had flown when Baba Yaga sat inside it. A dirty table stood in the middle of the room, and a fire burned in the grate, warming a cauldron filled with some lumpy sludge. The surface swirled with bubbles that burst with high-pitched squeals.

The witch raised her hand, and Leto rose through the air and came to rest on a rug before the stone fireplace. Her probing eyes found Zima. Black pupils glistened in eyes flecked with purple. The air around Zima grew cold, even with the fire burning, and she shifted uncomfortably under the witch's gaze.

"So, you'll do anything to save him . . . ," the witch said.

Zima's skin jumped. There was a hunger in the witch's words.

But then she spied her brother's limp paw, splayed across

the rug. This was no time for fear. She puffed out her chest and met the old crone's eyes without blinking.

The witch continued, "Then I'll grant your spell, if you grant mine."

Zima gasped. Her mouth was hot and her head light. *I do not understand . . .*

"I must become a wolf. Yet my magic does not allow me to simply transform. I am bound by the laws of the forest, and my magic is always a trade. I need a wolf to switch bodies with me, willingly." Her eyes brightened as she spoke.

Whatever Zima expected the witch to reply, it wasn't this. Let the witch have her body?

And if I give you my body, you will heal Leto?

The witch nodded.

A horrible thought struck Zima. If she agreed to switch places, Baba Yaga could pretend to be Zima. The witch could say anything, do anything, and everyone would assume it was Zima doing those things.

What about the rest of my family? Zima said, her panic rising. *You must stay away from them!*

"My plans do not involve your family," the witch said, her voice tinged with impatience. "Do we have a deal? Your brother does not have much time left."

Zima's breath came in short gasps. The air in the hut was so hot, it burned her lungs. She looked again at Leto's limp paw. She clenched her jaw and nodded.

"Good!" Baba Yaga declared. She slapped her hand against the table, causing Zima to jump.

Then the witch shuffled toward the fire and knelt down to examine Leto. She poked and prodded him, lifting his paw and letting it fall, jabbing him in the stomach and listening to him groan. . . . Zima moved to stop her, but Baba Yaga held up a hand.

"You brought him just in time. Any longer, and it would have been too late to save him."

Zima's heart missed a beat. *What do you mean?*

Baba Yaga straightened and began pulling jars from the shelves, and bunches of herbs and fungi from the rafters. She sprinkled them into a bowl, then used a wooden rod to grind them up. "My magic cannot create or destroy, it can only alter. I cannot kill, likewise I cannot create life where there is none." She lifted her gaze to Zima, her eyes heavy with meaning. "I cannot bring a wolf back from the dead."

Before Zima could respond, the witch was back to her work. With surprisingly delicate fingers, she scooped up the ground mixture and began applying it to Leto's wound. An earthy mushroom scent filled Zima's nostrils.

Is that the spell? Zima asked, curious in spite of herself.

"This?" Baba Yaga chuckled. "No, this is medicine. I do as much as I can without magic."

Why?

"My power comes from the earth, from this forest. It is

wild and untamable, and sometimes unpredictable. I am the riverbed, but the magic is the water. I can try to direct it, but sometimes it acts on its own."

She continued to apply the medicine to Leto as she spoke. Leto's breathing was slow, but it stayed steady.

"All I can do is ask the forest to save him. It does the rest."

Will the forest listen? Zima said.

"The forest is always listening, even to those who don't wield its magic," said Baba Yaga. "But magic is much easier to handle when you have what a spell needs," she said, a wicked smile twitching at her lips.

What does a spell need? Zima asked, trying to keep the eagerness out of her voice.

The witch chuckled, her eyes flashing at Zima before returning to Leto. "Heh ho, wouldn't you like to know? I don't want you doing magic in my body. You'll just hurt yourself."

Gripping her cane, the witch leaned closer to Leto and placed her other hand on his stomach, mumbling words under her breath. They sounded no more magical than a simple plea: "Please . . . heal him. . . ." The herbs crackled and sizzled. The rhythm of the witch's words was like a heartbeat. "Heal him, heal him. . . ." For some minutes there was nothing but the drone of her voice and the heat of the fire. Finally: silence.

The witch released her hand and turned to face Zima.

Baba Yaga's eyes were grim and determined. The table separated them, but she reached across it to place her hand on Zima's head, and before Zima could even say a word in response, Baba Yaga began to chant again.

Zima instinctively tried to duck away, but the witch jabbed her cane at Zima's side, and tightened her grip on Zima's head. Zima bit back the fear rising in her throat. She kept her eyes on Leto, watching his stomach rise and fall as he breathed, in and out, in and out.

Then, to Zima's amazement, her brother moved.

CHAPTER 18

Zima's head spun and the room blurred. For a moment she was lost in a thick fog, then Leto groaned, and her eyes cleared. Baba Yaga's grip on Zima's head loosened and fell away. The smell of magic, which had been overwhelming only a second before, had all but disappeared. But there was a strange new sense: a low hum seemed to buzz inside Zima, like whispers too soft for her to make out the words. The whispers filled her and flowed through her.

Zima darted forward to her brother. She nearly fell over her own strange new feet. Zima looked down. She stood on upright legs. Held out her arms and saw withered witch hands. She reached up and touched the leathery skin on her face and neck.

She looked with horror at the figure facing her. The witch had completely transformed into a wolf with Zima's exact silvery-gray coloring and the black streak along her back. Her paws rested casually on the table, her orange eyes cold.

The witch gave Zima a sharp look, and her wolf lips stretched into a satisfied grin. She leapt forward, around the table, her paws thumping on the wooden floor. In a voice that was like Zima's, but also sharper and older, she said, *Do not leave this hut while I am gone, do not admit any visitors. The humans cannot know that you are not the true Baba Yaga.*

Then she bounded through the door and down to the ground, disappearing from sight.

"Wait!" Zima shouted. The words scratched at her throat. She fumbled for the doorway and stood peering into the darkness. "How long will I be like this?"

The witch had abandoned her!

She could barely walk, knew nothing about magic, and had no knowledge of what the witch planned to do in her body.

But before she had time to panic, there was a cough behind her. She spun around, nearly losing her footing as her legs twisted together.

Leto gasped as though he'd been holding his breath since he'd been stabbed. He coughed and rolled onto his front of her face in defense and screamed, to no one in particular, "Help!"

The floor of the hut jolted beneath her feet, and Zima was thrown off-balance. Leto staggered sideways and crashed into the wall. He crumpled and fell, and then the splintered floorboards slid out from under him, leaving a gaping hole between Leto and the forest floor below. Leto tumbled through the hole to the ground, and the wooden floor slid back into place, shutting him out and blocking him from view.

Without warning, the whole house shuddered and shook. The herbs hanging from the ceiling swayed as jars, books, and skulls bounced on their shelves. Zima shuffled to the window and saw trees flashing past, the forest outside a blur. It took her a moment to realize that the house was running.

"Where are we going?" Zima cried. The voice that escaped from her mouth was dry and cracked, like the wooden wheels of village carts turning over the dirt and rocks of the road. "Wait—STOP!"

The house halted. Jars slid along the shelves but stopped before tumbling off, as if they were held by magic. From somewhere above her left shoulder, there came a squawk.

She turned around and tilted her chin up. On a bookshelf near the ceiling sat a raven, clicking his curved beak stomach. Horror slithered across his face as he took in the strangeness of the room and his eyes came to rest on Zima.

What have you done? he said to her, his voice small and shaking.

"S-saved you," Zima stammered.

But how did I get here? Where is Zima?

How could she explain? She struggled for the words, her new tongue heavy and dull. "Me . . . Baba Yaga . . . she's"—Zima gestured out the doorway, pointing where she last saw her own tail—"she disappeared." She shook her head, trying to force her mouth to form the words.

Leto pushed himself up onto his paws, then rounded on her. He seemed to have grown in size, and his features were warped into an expression Zima once saw Grom wear while fighting off a bear. He arched his back and bared his fangs. His side was still smeared with blood.

You have done something to her, he said, his voice rumbling. *You will regret this. . . .*

The words made Zima tremble. "Wait—I'm Zima!" she blurted out. "It's me!" Her hands thumped her chest.

Her brother stared at her, then bared his fangs once more. *I am not falling for your tricks.*

He swiped at her. Zima suddenly realized how frail a witch body was when faced with the fangs and claws of a wolf—even her little brother's. She threw her arms up i at her. He ruffled his glossy black feathers and squawked again.

"Quiet," snapped Zima. The whispers in her head and bones had swelled to a low chatter, and she fought to ignore them as she stepped forward to peek through the window. Nothing about the trees outside looked familiar. She sniffed, but the witch's nose could smell nothing. There was no way to tell where in the forest they were.

The raven flapped his wings. *Now you've done it,* he said. *Don't talk to anyone, don't leave the hut, and don't move the hut. You'll only break things.*

Zima's eyes snapped to the raven. "I . . . what?" she said, beginning to breathe very hard. She'd never been able to understand a raven before. It seemed that now that she was a witch, she could.

You asked for help. So the house . . . helped! He spoke the words very slowly, as though he expected Zima to struggle to understand them. He was right.

"But it didn't help! Baba Yaga changed me into a witch, and now the house has taken me somewhere, far from my family. This is worse! Much worse!"

Shh, don't let the house hear you. The raven looked up toward the rafters, as if checking for signs that the hut was angry. After a moment he seemed satisfied that they weren't overheard, and continued, *Fragile ego, this house. But very loyal. It will do anything and come from anywhere to help Baba Yaga, so long as she asks nicely.*

The raven hopped off the shelf and swooped down to stand on the table. *But I'm sorry to say it can't make you a wolf again.* He didn't sound sorry at all. He turned his head and began grooming himself, prodding his beak into his dark feathers. When he finished, he twirled to Zima and said cheerfully, *Though that brother of yours was going to make things worse than they are now, believe you me. You've been a witch for five minutes and you already have an enemy.*

His jolly tone pressed into her, and all at once the dangers of the day overwhelmed her. Zima collapsed into a chair. There was nothing, no Leto, no pack, no Veter, no one who knew the sacrifice she'd made. There was no going back.

Zima stared in silence at the fire. How had everything gone so wrong? This had been her best chance to prove she could protect their pack, and now she was cursed and separated from them. Grom would never have gotten into such a mess.

A tapping sound from the far corner made her start. The raven was cramming his beak into a cranny between the wall and the floor. When he noticed Zima staring, he said, *Beg pardon, don't let me interrupt your reverie. Was just hoping to catch this spider.* The spider, taking advantage of the raven's distraction, scurried from the nook, but the raven quickly snapped it up in his beak and swallowed.

"Do you know how I can change back?" Zima asked. She flexed her fingers and pinched the frayed ends of the wrap around her bony shoulders.

You can't, the raven said, still poking about the floor. *Only Baba Yaga can reverse the spell.*

"But Baba Yaga said there was something a spell needed . . . ," Zima said, half hoping, half expecting the raven to repeat it back to her. He didn't. She continued, "That there's some way to get the forest to listen to you." The raven still didn't speak. She staggered over to stand in front of him, nearly toppling over. The witch's cane wobbled as she leaned on it. She knelt down, so that her face was right in front of his. One of her knees made a popping sound. "Do you know how?"

The raven looked up, assessing her. He seemed ready to give a pert answer, but then shrugged. *Don't suppose it matters telling you. It requires an object. All witches have a magic object that allows them to channel power from the earth.*

Relief washed over Zima. She'd assumed magic would require something much more sinister. "And what is hers?"

The raven narrowed his eyes. *No trying to do magic.* He hopped onto an uppermost shelf and repeated, *Don't talk to anyone, don't leave the hut, don't move the hut, and don't try to do magic.* With a look up to the rafters he gave a dramatic sigh and said, to no one in particular, *I have too many things to do to include mothering this wolf on the list.* Then he prodded his beak into his wing once more, spitting out the bits of dirt that he plucked from between his feathers.

Zima swallowed. She could feel her temper rising, creeping up into her frizzy hair. But it wouldn't do to upset the raven; she needed an ally. She shoved the anger down again and fought to keep her voice steady. "Aren't you supposed to help the witch? That's me now. So you should help me."

Nice try, but I don't help people for free, you know. Not even Baba Yaga. I've already helped you without payment.

"How?" she asked.

I told you about needing the object. You can't expect me to find it for you too. Especially when she said she didn't want you doing magic. He continued preening. *No payment is worth defying orders.*

"Payment?" This was the second time he'd used that word. It wasn't something she'd heard of before. "What do you mean?"

The raven sighed. *It's when you give something to someone in exchange for what you want. You give me a gift, and I give you one.*

"Like a trade?"

Yes, exactly.

"What sort of payment?"

The raven cocked his head, thinking. *Favors, information. But when I can, I like to be paid in blackberries. Baba Yaga keeps an ever-ripe bush just for me.* He puffed up his feathers importantly.

Was this how the humans and Baba Yaga acted all the time? Zima tried to imagine a world where she only did things for others when they gave her something, and where she was only worried about what was best for herself instead of her pack. It left a foul taste on her tongue.

And anyway, the raven continued, *I don't know what her object is. She never told me, and the crafty old crone always seemed to use different objects when she performed spells, so I could never figure it out.*

Zima sank into a chair. She tried to picture what Baba Yaga had done when performing the spell, but her thoughts had been so focused on Leto, everything else was a blur.

How was she ever going to discover which of all the hundreds of jars, containers, knickknacks, and bits of clutter crowding the hut held the witch's powers? Now that she looked around, it almost seemed like the witch collected items for the purpose of making the task impossible. Various lanterns, vases, and piles of bones were tucked away in corners. On one small table was a bucket filled with nothing but rocks. It seemed like something the witch would do: choose an average, boring rock to hold her powers, and then keep it in a pile of other rocks.

As Zima searched, sometimes she could almost make out the words of the chattering whispers in her head, especially when she held certain objects, like a dagger she found tucked under the bed, and when she touched the enormous stone bowl. Yet those objects seemed no more magical than the soil stuck to her shoes. It seemed that whatever it was the voices had to say, it wasn't how to do magic or become a wolf again.

She longed for her wolf nose. She could have sniffed out the object in an instant. It was a marvel that witches were able to do anything with such a terrible sense of smell.

Her old body creaked as she moved a few steps to investigate the next shelf. Having hands, though, was a welcome change, even ones that ached and throbbed as she flexed the fingers. It was nice to be able to pick up jars without using her mouth.

But the next object she picked up, a vase, slipped from between her fingers, which were not yet used to gripping and holding. The vase shattered on the wooden floor, and the pieces that remained were sharp as teeth. The raven sighed and gestured to an object, a long and sturdy branch with a bunch of grass and twigs tied to its end, leaning against the wall near the door. At first Zima couldn't see how the bundle of sticks would help. But after the raven snapped at her that it was called a broom, that she was holding it upside down and told her how to use it, she was able to sweep the shards of the vase into one of the witch's empty buckets.

She collapsed on the witch's bed. The wooden slats squeaked under her weight. "So you won't help me find my magic object, but you will help me learn how to use a broom?" she said, failing to keep the bitterness out of her voice.

The last thing I need is to cut my toe chasing a spider, said the raven haughtily. *And you are much better equipped to use that broom than I am.*

Zima curled into a ball, wishing she could wrap her tail around herself. Lying down in this body wasn't very comfortable; it was no wonder Baba Yaga slept on a bed. Her feet throbbed. Her breaths were ragged and shallow. The whispers were an endless drone, making her head feel foggy and slow. Baba Yaga was every bit as evil as she'd always heard, for leaving Zima alone in this perplexing body in her unfamiliar hut.

CHAPTER 19

Nadya sat in the dirt outside the orphanage, her back to the wall, and the doll splayed in her lap for closer inspection. It was made of wood, with whittled head, hands, and legs, and wrapped in a woven flax dress. It was an ugly thing, with half its grass hair falling out and its tiny clothes in tatters. She hadn't held a doll in years, but something about its painted smile was comforting.

A breeze ripped past her, dancing through the doll's hair before rushing to tug dry leaves from the branches of the trees lining the edge of the forest. Six days—that's all the time she had left before her life changed. She just had to prove that she was worthy of joining Katerina in the castle.

She pulled the doll closer, as if Katerina's wisdom and

instruction might somehow rub off. Yet as she held it, something seemed amiss. It was hard to put into thoughts or words, too silly to even think of saying. Though if she let her thoughts speak the truth, she would admit: the doll felt almost . . . alive.

She looked at it again more closely. Did the smile seem expressive? No, that wasn't it. Maybe she could feel Katerina's love for this childhood toy, as though it had burrowed its way into the doll's body.

But it made her feel uneasy too, like the doll was watching her. She couldn't shake the feeling that it had life pulsing beneath its wooden skin. And then, for a moment, she thought she heard a whisper.

Nadya dropped the doll with a yelp of surprise.

She was imagining things.

Pinching its little hand between her fingers, she gingerly picked up the doll. Though she knew she was imagining things, she still wasn't eager to touch it. She took the stairs two at a time as she returned to the room she shared with the other girls. It was empty—everyone was probably still out in the village, enjoying the excitement of seeing Katerina in her finery in the tsar's carriage. The only sound was the squeak of the floorboards under her feet. Nadya worked to step more lightly, knowing it's what Katerina would want from a perfectly behaved girl.

But what to do with the doll? She didn't like looking at

it, so for the time being she slid it under her lumpy pillow out of view.

With a last glance behind her, she left to finish her chores. If she had any hope of proving to Mrs. Orlova that she could go to the castle, she must do everything that was expected of her *before* she was asked, and with no mistakes.

Later that night, when Nadya returned to the room and prepared for bed, the doll sat on a table next to the window, its head leaning against the glass as though it were looking out at the forest. Mrs. Orlova must have picked it up and set it there, though Nadya was sure she hadn't seen the matron enter the room all day.

CHAPTER 20

Zima snatched another bottle from the shelf, straining her ears to decipher the murmuring voices around her. She wanted to find the magic object and restore herself to her wolf body as soon as possible. The voices continued to mutter and jabber, but gave no indication that this item was more magical than any of the other items she'd held.

She returned the vial to the shelf, and her belly gave an irritated grumble. She'd been ignoring the pangs of hunger all morning, but at this point her stomach seemed to be threatening to eat itself.

There were herbs and mushrooms hanging from the rafters, but the mushrooms weren't ones Zima knew. They might be poisonous. She grabbed a bit of dill, an herb she recognized, and began to nibble it. But if she was going to be stuck as a witch for much longer, she would have to find something more substantial to eat.

The fire still burned, and over it hung the enormous cauldron. She stared at the fire, a cold dread prickling in her chest. This fire wasn't like the one that had ravaged the trees and ripped her family apart. When her father had taken her to the edge of the village all those moons ago, he had explained how humans knew how to tame fire and control it—how they used it for things like cooking and warmth. She would have to trust that this fire wasn't the wild, untamable kind she'd seen in the past.

She peered inside the cauldron, where gray sludge bubbled. Maybe the sludge was some sort of food? It smelled like it might be edible, with hints of honey and sage, though it was hard to tell with this terrible witch nose. Her gnarled finger touched the surface of the liquid. *Ouch!* Was human food always this hot? She seized a wooden rod with a rounded end that hung on a hook nearby, and was just poking out her tongue for a small taste when—

I wouldn't do that, if I were you, said the raven. He shook his feathers and blinked at her sleepily from his nook in the rafters.

"What is it?"

Not food.

Zima groaned. "Can't you just tell me?"

I could, but I don't see why I should.

Zima shoved the stick back on the hook, where it clattered against the stone wall of the fireplace. "Then why did you tell me not to eat it? Why tell me *some* things and not others?"

The raven swooped over to the windowsill and began poking with his beak at the latch holding it closed. *Because if you ate it and then died here in the hut, I'd have to find a way to drag you outside. Last thing I need is a dead body that's too big for me to move.*

It was hard to tell whether he really meant this. She couldn't believe he was so uncaring. A low growl rumbled in her throat. "Well, if I die of starvation, you'll be stuck with my body anyway," she snapped.

The raven glared at her, then jabbed his beak at a set of shelves. *You can eat anything in those sacks. And she uses the cauldron for scrying.*

Zima plunked a hand into a brown cloth bag and yanked out some sort of knobbly root. Her stomach groaned, and she bit into it. It crunched, and a warm, spicy flavor made her mouth tingle.

"There, now, was that so hard?" she said to the raven, smiling. Flecks of the root leapt from her mouth as she tried to talk and chew at the same time. Then she asked, "What's scrying?" She'd never heard that word before.

It shows visions of things.

"What sorts of visions?"

The raven let out a dramatic sigh. *Nothing you need to know about.*

Zima matched his sigh, making it as dramatic as possible. "You can't expect me to sit here forever, not knowing what she's doing in my body. I need to know *something*!"

I've told you plenty of things. I just told you what food to eat and what the cauldron does.

"But you haven't told—"

The raven flapped his wings and squawked in agitation. *Fine, fine,* he sighed, *I'll tell you! But if you whine again, I won't answer a single other question, understood?*

Zima pressed her hands together eagerly.

Pick up the spoon.

"The what?"

He flapped his wings again. *The wooden thing. You were just holding it.*

Zima moved back toward the cauldron and plucked the spoon from the hook on the wall. The surface of the liquid was steaming. The grayish-brown of wild mushrooms looked almost green when she turned her head. Bubbles grew and burst with mouselike squeaks. Stirring the surface of the liquid per his instructions, she leaned forward to inhale the earthy and smoky scents.

It can only show you her memories, said the raven, *so ask it about something Baba Yaga would remember.*

"So it can't show me where she is now? Or how to become a wolf again?" Disappointment nibbled at Zima's insides. She had hoped the cauldron would help her reverse Baba Yaga's spell.

The raven shook his head. *Ask it why you're here,* he said.

As Zima leaned forward to speak the words, the whispers she'd heard ever since becoming Baba Yaga skittered like spiders over her skin. They grew and spread, until she was covered in them, her whole body wriggling and humming. Her eyes filled with smoke from the fire.

When the smoke cleared and the whispers lowered to their usual hum, Baba Yaga was seated at the table in front of her, drinking steaming liquid from a mug. Zima jumped. Had the witch returned?

But Baba Yaga didn't seem to notice Zima at all. Zima held up her withered hands. They were the witch's hands. She was still in Baba Yaga's body, with the raven perched on her shoulder. And yet Baba Yaga was also seated right in front of her.

A memory, just as the raven had said. She was in Baba Yaga's memory.

Wind howled over the roof and past the chimney. The firelight gave the room a soft glow that must have been the only light visible in the forest for many miles.

The first knock on the door was no louder than a tree branch scratching against the window. The second was louder, more desperate, and by the time the witch had risen and tugged a wool cloth over her shoulders, the third knock was nearly strong enough to break the door down.

Muttering curses to herself, Baba Yaga went to the door.

The latch gave a soft click as she undid it and began to turn the handle. Then a gust of wind caught the door and blew it wide open.

On the threshold stood a young couple, the woman clutching a crying baby in her arms. The firelight threw shadows on their threadbare clothes and holey shoes.

With arms folded across her chest, the witch said to the visitors, "Were you forced to come here, or did you choose to come?" It was the same thing Baba Yaga had said to Zima. It must be what she said to every visitor.

The woman stammered out a response. "We ch-chose to come. The b-baby—" she began.

But the man cut her off. "We found this child," he said. "In the forest."

The wife's breath caught in her throat. She looked swiftly down at the child, avoiding Baba Yaga's gaze. Then she jiggled the baby and made a cooing sound to soothe it.

Baba Yaga reached out to the baby. But the woman pulled away, clutching the child close to her chest. The abrupt motion led to a new waterfall of wails from the infant.

"He's sick, I don't know what's wrong," said the wife. "I was hoping you could—"

"That child belongs to me," the witch said, fire and thunder rolling deep in her voice.

At these words, the woman's eyes grew wide with fright. She stumbled away from Baba Yaga, out the door of the hut and down the steps to the forest floor. Her husband followed close behind, his shouts for her to come back lost in the wind.

Standing at the door of the hut, Baba Yaga stretched out a hand, fingers spread wide like bat wings. "Stop!" she commanded.

Through the window, Zima watched in horror as roots tore from the earth, sending snow and mud into the air. They twisted around the woman's ankles, just as they had done to Zima in her own first encounter with the witch. The woman lurched and nearly lost her grip on the baby, but managed to hold fast.

But so did the roots. They tied the woman in place. She squirmed, trying to rip her legs free.

Slowly Baba Yaga descended the steps. Her feet seemed to glide across the snow as she moved toward them, stopping where the man stood next to the trapped young woman. In her voice were all the depths of the earth, the fury of an earthquake. "Do not run again," she charged. "I will give you one spell, and one spell only, in exchange for the child. I will not offer again."

The man reached out and took the baby from his wife's

arms, his own hands trembling. The woman screamed and collapsed into the snow, her hair catching on the twigs and brambles surrounding her.

Holding the baby close, the man said, "The spell I— we—request is for my family to be able to come to you with a question—any question—and be assured of a truthful answer." The child's cries quieted, as though he too was eager for the witch's spell.

Zima couldn't help but feel impressed. Grom said humans always lied, but this one was on a search for truth.

"Done," said Baba Yaga, with a glance at the full moon overhead. "The full moon seals the exchange. I will give you and your family truth, always." She extended her arms toward him. "Now give me the child."

The man's lips quirked, and he looked down at the now-cooing baby. "How do I know that the exchange is sealed? I should ask a question first, so I know."

Baba Yaga's jaw tightened, but she nodded. "Then, what is your question?" she asked.

The look the man gave her was full of venom. "How do I become the tsar?" he asked.

It wasn't a word Zima recognized, but she could feel the hunger in the man's voice as he said it.

Baba Yaga clamped her mouth closed, and Zima watched as she struggled against the powers of the moon and earth that bound her. Only when she seemed close to snapping like a bough in a lightning storm did she speak, in a voice that was not her own. It seemed to come from somewhere different entirely, somewhere beyond them both. The voice told the man of a tunnel that led from the forest to a castle, which would allow them to sneak inside the castle undetected. It spoke of how the current tsar loved to play chess, and of a dagger of gold and rubies that could be found in the tsar's room and used to murder him while he played.

None of this made any sense . . . castle, chess, tsar. . . . But one word Zima did recognize: "murder."

Zima could feel Baba Yaga's heartache as the witch spoke. The horrible instructions made her breathless. This man was going to kill someone. "But know this," said Baba Yaga, "if you kill him, then that dagger is cursed. It will seek the blood of a tsar, always."

The man was unfazed. His jaw jutted forward and he stared at Baba Yaga, as if challenging her to stop him.

She extended her arms for the child, her palms wet from the tears streaming down her cheeks.

With a smile, the man held the baby out to her.

As moonlight illuminated the child, an unreadable expression flickered across Baba Yaga's face. She stepped away from both man and baby, and before the man had time to protest, she had retreated into her hut, leaving the child in his arms.

As Baba Yaga shut the door behind her, the whispers in

Zima's head swelled louder than ever. They filled her ears and throat and chest, rumbling as though the ground beneath her feet were shaking. *Find the gray wolf,* the voices said. *Find the gray wolf.* She could almost taste the words. Almost touch the voices that Zima knew, without understanding why, came from the very forest itself. *Find the gray wolf. Find the gray wolf.* By the look on Baba Yaga's face, she guessed that the witch could hear them too.

But in the memory, Baba Yaga didn't find the gray wolf. Instead, she sat by the warm fire, returning to the drink she'd been sipping only a few minutes before.

"I don't understand," said Zima. "Why did she agree?"

She had to take the child by any means necessary, said the raven, sorrow weighing down his words. *A baby found in the forest, growing like a root, is a new witch. One is born when it will soon be time for this Baba Yaga's reign to end.* He turned very grave. *She has to raise it to become the next Baba Yaga.*

"But she didn't." Baba Yaga had let the humans take the baby away.

He lied, said the raven. *It was an ordinary human. She didn't realize until after she'd agreed to the bargain. He had risked his own child in order to get what he wanted.* The raven croaked. *Despicable.*

"But why didn't she stop him? He wanted to *murder* someone."

Fear, he said. *That he or any other human would trick her again. She chose to conceal herself, to avoid humans at all costs. And for a hundred years, she did.*

One hundred years? It was an old memory. All those years ago the human had tricked the witch into helping him murder another human, and Baba Yaga had done nothing to stop it. She'd let fear stop her.

And now she'd tricked Zima into becoming a part of some cryptic scheme.

Zima wanted no part of this. Whatever role she was playing in this scene from Baba Yaga's past, it had nothing to do with Zima now. But what could she do? Anything was better than waiting here, trapped in this hut, vulnerable to any other humans who came along looking for spells.

She had moved half a step toward the door when a noise from outside startled both her and the raven. There was a crash as something pounded against the chicken legs of the hut, then a thrashing of bushes and twigs.

Someone was prowling about on the ground below.

CHAPTER 21

aba Yaga stretched her legs, feeling their power, the muscles and balance that allowed her to leap over the uneven ground as if she were flying.

She held the scent of the dagger in her nose. The wolf's senses were stronger than her witch body's had been—even at the height of her powers—and her new nose was her guide. The blade still remembered the blood of the old tsar, and Baba Yaga had breathed it with her new wolf sense of smell. She would hunt them. The sooner she found them, the sooner the task of defeating the tsar would fall to someone else instead of herself.

Though it had been many years since the dagger had tasted blood, the scent still lingered. It was a subtle kind of magic, but one she could take advantage of as a wolf. The fact that she'd managed to get hold of the dagger at all was a wonder. It certainly made her glad for the raven's assistance.

But even with the valuable clue from the dagger, finding her prey still required her to catch a hint of their scent somewhere.

The first part of her journey was to travel to the great road, the one that connected the villages on the edge of the forest to the city beyond. The shortest way was through the depths of the forest.

As much as she enjoyed her new wolf senses, there was an emptiness inside her that grew increasingly hard to ignore as she ran deeper into the forest's heart.

She had never been separated from her magic object before. It had connected her life force to the forest. Were her witch body to go too long without it, she would die. For the first time in three hundred years, she could no longer hear the voices of the forest. When she strained her ears and looked deep inside herself, she thought perhaps she could hear them. But they were no more tangible than a soft breeze.

The emptiness distracted her, clawed at her as she leapt down a hill toward a stream. It was too late by the time she realized what the stream was.

The sound of the water should have told her. The omen that tolled under its bubbling current.

These were the Waters of Death.

She snapped her mouth closed, realizing her mistake just as she plunged into the stream. Touching it wouldn't kill her—in fact, the waters could heal some injuries—but if she swallowed even a drop, her heart would stop beating.

What a fool she was! Overlooking, ignoring.

This was her forest, and yet she hadn't heeded what it told her.

It had been so long since she'd listened. Because she hadn't wanted to hear. And now she had almost met her death within moments of beginning her journey.

She shook herself dry. The air threatened snow. She had to remember the secrets of the forest, evade its tricks and perils.

With careful steps, Baba Yaga continued on her journey. She would not be caught unawares again.

CHAPTER 22

*O*h *dear,* said the raven.

"What?" said Zima, snapping to attention. She'd been thinking of Grom, wondering if the pack was safe, if they were worried about her. "Who is it?"

The raven stared at her, as if he'd never heard such a foolish question before.

Someone desperate for a spell, I expect. Why else would anyone dare disturb Baba Yaga?

Zima moved away from the window. What if the human tried to trick her into giving something she didn't want to give, like the man in the memory? Her hands clutched at her bony cheeks. "But I can't do spells!" she said in a nervous whisper. "I haven't found the object yet. And Baba

Yaga said I mustn't talk to anyone!" She wanted to tuck her tail between her legs—if only she still had a tail.

Quiet! shushed the raven. *Just stay hidden and they might think you're not home.* He craned his neck to the top of the windowpane, his beak flattened against the glass, looking down at the ground.

"Get away from there!" said Zima. "What if they see you?"

I'm just trying to get a look, said the raven in a guarded voice. His shoulders were hunched. *If I say RUN, tell the hut to get us out of here.*

"What?! How?" said Zima.

Shush! I can see something. . . .

Nothing the raven said was comforting. In fact, each time he spoke, it made the whole situation seem worse.

No . . . it's . . . not a human, said the raven.

The pounding of her heart in her ears lessened slightly. "What did you say?"

I said it's not a human. It's . . . The raven pulled away from the window and rolled his eyes at her. *It's a wolf.*

Zima scrambled toward the window and stretched up on the tips of her toes to look down at the creature below. It took less than a second to recognize the skipping walk and brown shoulders of Veter.

Her temper erupted, engulfing the terror that had just possessed her. So *now* Veter decided he could come to the witch? He managed to muster the courage, only after it was too late and Zima was trapped in a witch's body.

"House!" Zima shouted as she stomped to the door and grasped the handle. "When I say so, get us out of here and kick some dirt in Veter's face while you're at it!"

The raven opened his beak to protest that Baba Yaga had ordered her not to speak to anyone, but Zima had thrown the door open. The house gave a nervous shudder, as though it was letting her open the door against its better judgment.

"What are you doing here?" she snapped at the figure on the ground.

Veter's ears twitched and folded back. He looked up at her, his brow furrowed and his paws planted firmly on the ground. Zima could tell he was trying to act braver than he felt. When he spoke, his voice shook.

I am looking for Zima.

"Why?" Zima said, glaring at him.

Because I need to make sure she is unharmed.

Part of Zima's heart was touched that he had faced his fears to come looking for her. But it was a small part. The bigger part remembered that she probably wouldn't be in this mess if he hadn't abandoned her yesterday.

For a second she wished that she had the witch's magic object in hand, so she could switch places with Veter. At least she'd be in a wolf body, though not her own, and Veter would be the one stuck as a witch.

Instead, she said, "She's gone. You won't find her, so don't bother looking."

There was just time for Veter to let out a pitiful whimper before Zima slammed the door closed and threw herself into a chair.

The boom of the door shook the walls. When the rattling ceased, the raven said dryly, *Well, that was unnecessary.*

Zima ignored him. "House!" she shouted. "Get us out of here! And don't forget what I said about the dirt!"

But the hut didn't move.

"House!" Zima said again.

Nothing acknowledged her words. No creak of wooden rafters, no tilting floor to signify a nod.

"Why doesn't it answer?" Zima asked the raven.

Maybe it doesn't like being yelled at.

He stared at her, his beak lifted smugly, and Zima deflated a little, ashamed of herself. She held her head in her hands for a moment. She shouldn't have lost her temper like that, not at Veter and especially not at the house. There was no one she could turn to for help when she needed it. "Oh, what should I do?" she asked.

The raven gave a pointed look up at the rafters. A musty, grassy scent floated downward from the hanging herbs. *I've told you, you have to ask nicely.*

"No, I mean . . . ," said Zima, peeking between her fingers, "about Veter . . ."

Ah, said the raven. He puffed up his feathers. *Well, that's not really my concern.*

Zima ignored him. The unhelpful little feather-beast. She had to make it up to Veter for yelling at him. He clearly regretted his decision and had come to set things right. And Zima had told him her wolf self was gone, all but saying outright that it was his fault.

She pushed herself upright and skulked back to the door. It opened with a creak. On the grass below, Veter sat, unmoving, his head hung low.

"Veter," Zima called.

He lifted his head. The sunlight caught the long scar across his face. He narrowed his eye at her.

How do you know my name?

Zima coughed. She thought she heard a titter of laughter from the raven behind her, and waved her hand at him to be quiet. "I . . . er . . . I'm a witch," she said. She placed her hands on her hips. "Of course I know."

And why will I not find Zima? Veter asked, getting straight to the point. *What have you done with her?* His lips curled into the hint of a snarl.

For a moment Zima was glad of the distance that separated them. Something in the angle of Veter's ears and the stiffening of his tail told her that he really was ready to attack her witch body if it meant coming to the rescue of her wolf self. But she didn't need him to come to her rescue, and she certainly didn't need to be attacked.

"She's fine. Zima is fine," Zima said.

The tension that had pulled Veter's whole body tight seemed to visibly loosen. He breathed out in relief. *But where is she? I want to see her.*

"She's on a mission," Zima said. It seemed like the closest thing she could say to the truth.

Veter's ears drooped. *When will she return?* he asked.

"I don't know."

Oh, Veter said. *I hoped* . . . But what it was he'd hoped, he didn't say.

"What is it?" Zima said. The softness in her voice surprised her. It was like the creaking of trees in a spring breeze.

I hoped she might help me . . . *to become part of her pack.* For a moment the sadness that hung over him blew away, and his face brightened, like the sun peeking through storm clouds. But then he drooped again. *I went to them after the human hurt Leto, but when Grom found out I left Zima, he was furious. He sent me away.*

Veter wanted a pack. He had no one. Why had she never thought of this before? She had been so focused on her own problems she'd never even thought about the challenges Veter faced. He had gone through the same pain of losing his parents. Worse, even, because he'd lost his entire family. At least Zima had had her brothers to distract and comfort her.

"Are they safe?" Zima asked.

Yes, I think so. But . . . Veter hesitated, looking down at his paws.

"But what?"

I worry that things are going to get worse between the wolves and the humans. I do not know if it is safe for me in the village anymore.

Zima moved to meet his gaze. She stared at him long and hard, hoping that he could see something in her eyes. For a second she considered telling him everything. That the witch had forced her to trade places in exchange for Leto's life. That she didn't know how to change back. That her only guidance came from the infuriating raven, who gave her half advice and usually did so grudgingly.

"I fear that too," Zima said at last. He was right. He couldn't stay in the village anymore. "Zima wants her pack to go somewhere deep in the forest, away from the humans. You should go too."

Me alone, deep in the forest? Veter's ears drooped and his tail curled.

Zima remembered how her fear of Baba Yaga first gave her the idea to run away to find somewhere safe. Fear was also what had kept Baba Yaga from stopping a murder. But maybe a little fear would help Veter, would motivate him to find safety.

She puffed out her chest and tried to summon all the danger that Baba Yaga's voice had held in the cauldron's memory. "Don't make me curse you . . . ," she said. "Leave the village, find somewhere to hide. Do as I say!"

Veter yipped and began to back away.

In a softer tone she added, "When Zima returns, she will find you."

When he turned to leave, Zima watched him until she could see only the memory of his tail slipping away between the trees.

But Veter wasn't the only visitor to Baba Yaga's hut. The next day there came another. This time, a human.

CHAPTER 23

If there were moments when Nadya wasn't thinking about moving to the castle in the wake of Katerina's departure, she would be hard pressed to say when they were. Her mind was constantly looking for ways to impress, ways to improve, ways to convince Mrs. Orlova that she deserved so grand a home.

She had cooked and cleaned without complaint, even going so far as to scrub the floors with lye that burned her hands and stung her eyes. The old woman had watched Nadya with narrowed eyes, clearly looking to find fault: Had Nadya used enough lye? Was she scrubbing against the grain of the wood? But after a few moments of watching in silence, Mrs. Orlova moved on to scrutinize the other girls.

Mrs. Orlova said everyone in the village was expected to offer Katerina and the tsar a wedding gift, including those in the orphanage. But for Nadya it was more than a gift. If Katerina could win over the tsar with her weaving, then maybe Nadya's gift could win over the tsar too.

Nadya gripped a length of fabric with tense fingers. For the first time she found herself wishing she'd tried harder to learn the skills Mrs. Orlova had given up on teaching her. There was nothing she could offer that would earn the tsar's favor. She'd tried baking already, but her cake was flat and grainy. And her attempts at painting were not much better. She was now trying to embroider a pattern of leaves, but they looked more like lumpy twigs—she'd never gotten the hang of the elegant dance between needle and fabric that came so naturally to some girls.

With a groan Nadya pressed her palms to her eyes. She'd been staring at the tangles and knots for too long. She needed a breath of air.

Her muscles ached as she gave Mrs. Orlova a bow and the excuse that she was just stepping outside momentarily in hopes of finding some leaves to inspire her embroidery. Mrs. Orlova craned her neck a little, clearly interested in taking a look at the girl's progress, but Nadya crumpled the fabric in her fists so that the old woman couldn't see.

She breathed in the dry scent of the leaves. She had to be careful not to stray too close to the forest—she didn't want

Mrs. Orlova to think she had wandered off again. Instead, taking a seat on an old tree stump, she enjoyed the taste of the wintry air on her tongue and its metallic chill against her ears.

As she peered toward the trees, a familiar eye blinked at her. Nadya stood, nearly dropping her work into the mud, but she managed to catch it just in time.

"No, no," she said out loud. Now was not the time for her wolf to visit, not when Mrs. Orlova was watching her so closely. She waved her arms at him. "Shoo!" she said. "Go away!"

Her wolf was undeterred. He slunk closer. His movements were different from before, more cautious, almost fearful. He crept toward her, then back, toward her and back, almost as if he wanted her to follow him.

But that wouldn't do. She had promised to stay out of the woods.

She waved her fabric at him, hoping it would convince him to go. Instead, he jumped up and snatched it in his jaws, the force of his grip pulling her to her feet.

"Stop!" Nadya hissed at him. *"Please!"*

But he didn't understand. The harder she tried to pull it away from him, the more he tugged, until there was a horrible tearing sound.

A scream slashed through the air. "Get away from that beast!" shouted Mrs. Orlova. She rushed forward and yanked Nadya back by the shoulders.

The force of Mrs. Orlova's grip made Nadya lose hold of the fabric, and she fell, leaving the shreds of the ruined wedding gift in her wolf's mouth. He spat it on the ground and approached Nadya again. There was no anger visible in his eye, but something else. Was it fear? She was sure now that there was something he was trying to tell her.

But she couldn't listen. She let Mrs. Orlova pull her toward the orphanage.

"What in heaven's name were you doing?" snapped the matron once they were safe inside the kitchen. "That creature could have dragged you into the forest!"

Nadya shook her head. "He wouldn't . . . ," she began, though part of her wondered if that was exactly what he was trying to do.

Mrs. Orlova ignored her protest. "How Katerina could

have ever thought that you could behave well enough to be a guest at the castle," she spat. "Now with no gift . . . and look at the state of you!"

Some of the other girls nearby giggled as Nadya looked down. At some point during the tussle with her wolf she had managed to rip her dress and get dirty smudges across the clean white cloth.

"Oh, Nadya, that settles it," Mrs. Orlova said. "There's little hope of you living in the castle. I'm going to write to Mr. Demidov."

The woman swept from the room, leaving Nadya surrounded by the whispers of the other girls, whispers that crawled under her skin and lodged in her brain, as whispers loved to do. Without a word Nadya ran up the stairs, angry tears threatening to spill out of her eyes.

In two steps she had retrieved her warm woolen cloak and red head scarf. Her map and a small knife went into her bag. There was little else she would need in the forest. She would eat the berries and roots that she could find and make her way to the city in the south. It was her only option now.

An ache tugged at her insides. With Katerina's invitation, she had been so close to having a home, and someone who *wanted* her. And now she would be alone again. There would be no way to convince the tsar to let her stay, not when Mrs. Orlova gave news of what had happened.

If only she had something to give the tsar that would

force him to grant her a favor in return as he had offered marriage in exchange for Katerina's cloak. But it had to be something extraordinary that would leave him no choice but to provide the home she sought. If only she had such a thing. It would mean she could live with Katerina even though she had done everything else wrong.

Of course, that was impossible. She had nothing. And there was nothing the tsar lacked; he had within easy grasp anything he could ever wish for.

Wish.

Wish.

The word tickled Nadya's nose. There was one thing the tsar lacked: magic.

The witch. Baba Yaga. If Nadya could offer him something magical, something that fulfilled his deepest wish, he would be bound by the traditions of the forest to give her her dearest wish in exchange.

Nadya shivered. Only those who were terribly desperate ever sought out the witch. Was she that desperate?

She could try her luck in the forest, and make her way through the deadly traps and coming winter ice toward the city, and try to find a new home there. Her map would show her the way. Or she could seek out the witch. Both options were dangerous, both possibly even *deadly.*

She had braved the forest many times. She could brave a witch too.

Her mind made up, Nadya hurried down the stairs past the other girls, their curious glances and muttered words pricking her like thorns. They called out for Mrs. Orlova as Nadya stepped through the kitchen door and into the new sharp wind that swept along the forest's edge.

Trees peered over the little hillock beyond the barn and henhouse. Without waiting for fear to overtake her, Nadya crossed the hill to the shadowy space where the trees began.

It was said that anyone resigned enough to seek Baba Yaga would be guided to her hut by the forest itself, as if by magic. In this, Nadya hoped that the stories were true. She took a deep breath. She couldn't know if Baba Yaga would help her, but it was worth the risk. Now that she had tasted the possibility of belonging somewhere, she couldn't let it go.

Without even a final glance at the village or the faces of those she was leaving behind, Nadya took a step forward and entered the darkness of the forest, thinking only of her desire to find the witch.

CHAPTER 24

Dread filled Zima's stomach once more as she listened to the crunching footsteps of the human creeping toward the hut. But when the human stepped into a patch of sunlight, a flash of red caught Zima's eye and she recognized the little girl—the one she was supposed to kill.

Not for the first time, she wished she had Grom's steady presence beside her, to calm and protect her.

Baba Yaga had told Zima not to speak to any humans. Now was the time to ask the hut to take her somewhere else. She opened her mouth to say the words, but curiosity tugged at her. This was the second time she'd seen this girl, this human, in only a few days, and the first time was right before the witch arrived. It was unlikely, but part of her wondered if talking to the girl would help her find out how to become a wolf again. The muttered voices in Zima's head seemed to agree, though it was hard to be sure when they kept talking over each other.

The raven was out. He'd left early that morning to deliver some secret message for Baba Yaga. He wouldn't know.

She could pretend to be Baba Yaga just as she had with Veter, say the words the witch had said, gesture the way she had gestured. If the human didn't know the difference, the witch would never find out that Zima had spoken to anyone.

The hut lowered itself to the ground with a *thump,* and the wooden steps creaked down to the forest floor as Zima opened the door.

Zima swallowed hard. The thought of trying to have a conversation with a human made her insides writhe like dying snakes, but she had to be brave. The witch was feared throughout the whole forest. No one would do anything to her.

"Were you forced to come here," she said, imitating the witch's words, "or did you choose to come?" It made her feel braver, more powerful, to say them.

The little girl tugged on the red cloth covering her head. "I chose," she said, her voice shaking, as though she weren't used to using it. "My name is Nadya, and I need your help."

CHAPTER 25

There was so little time. Four nights remained until the full moon. If Baba Yaga couldn't complete her plans by then, all would be lost.

The first village teemed with people preparing for the coming winter. The *thunk* and *clang* of axes rang through the air as humans chopped firewood, and the odor of boiled cabbage and brewed kvass was thick enough to taste. She circled the village, searching for a hint of the scent she needed. But no human, each with a distinctive smell, matched that of the dagger.

The next village was only a half day from the first.

But the village after that was a full day's run from the second.

With each night Baba Yaga watched the moon grow fatter. Five nights left. Now four. Soon three. The moon regarded her but could provide no assistance. Neither could the forest. She was alone, and only she could find the family.

The pads of her paws were split from running. She could hardly bring herself to circle the next village. The villagers, with their friendly chatter and scampering children, tried her patience and overwhelmed her sensitive ears. Being around so many people—more people than she had seen in all three hundred years of her lifetime—was exhausting. The only thing keeping her legs running was the thought of returning to the solitude of her hut.

After dodging a hunter who had glimpsed her circling his village, she was close to collapsing.

But then something made her nose twitch. A hint of a scent on the wind. Her breath caught in her throat.

Somewhere nearby was the smell she was looking for.

She doubled back in among the trees, letting their branches conceal her. Weaving between ferns and leaping over logs, Baba Yaga made her way toward the road that hugged the perimeter of the forest.

She was more confident than ever in her ability to navigate the forest. The deadly flowers no longer surprised her, now that she'd begun to recognize their odors. Since her slip-up with the stream, she had evaded all other dangers; she was almost pleased with herself.

But she'd congratulated herself too soon. So focused was she on the scent that she leapt over a log without looking. Her paws landed on dry leaves. With a crackle they collapsed beneath her weight and she tumbled into a hole, her wolf body slapping against earth and roots and finally striking hard stone. For a moment she lay motionless. Her legs shook and her chest ached.

Baba Yaga forced herself to breathe in and out, trying to calm the throbbing radiating from her stomach to her limbs. In and out. In and out.

At last, her breaths slowed and she moved a paw. It shook a little, but nothing seemed to be broken or sprained. She put weight on the paw and rolled over, heaving herself onto her feet.

Her eyes had adjusted to the darkness as she'd lain there. A cave opened out before her. But frustration stilled her paws. Once more, her own forest had surprised her. She'd failed in navigating it.

With cautious steps she ventured into the quiet of the cave.

But all was not silent. Scuffling creatures surrounded her. Her wolf senses could pick up the heartbeats of mice and voles burrowing through the soil nearby. She could feel their tiny eyes watching her nervously. If only she were still a witch, they would have helped her out of this trap. . . .

But would they?

Or would they have feared her witch form just as much as her wolf one? She had been callous and uncaring toward the creatures of the forest, apart from her raven. These animals would have no desire to help her escape. It was no wonder the wolf only agreed to trade places with her when she was desperate and had no other choice.

She looked up. Roots dangled from the ceiling of the cave, glittering with ice. It was beautiful. She had never before glimpsed this view of the forest.

Baba Yaga stood watching it, enjoying the way the soft breeze in the cave made the ice chime with its own music. But a scent on the breeze made her snap to attention.

The human. It was nearer.

She scrambled toward the shaft she'd tumbled down and let out a whining howl. Her sensitive ears picked up footsteps. She moaned and howled again.

"What is that? Where are you?" called a male voice.

Baba Yaga moaned again.

A shadow fell across the hole from the surface. A young man with straw-colored hair, no more than sixteen years old, peered down.

"Oh!" he said in stunned concern. "Are you hurt?" He clearly didn't expect an answer, but Baba Yaga whimpered back at him.

"Hold, hold right there," he said, waving at her. He disappeared for a moment, then reappeared with a length of rope, which he lowered toward her. "Can you grab that with your teeth?" he asked.

Baba Yaga hesitated. If she allowed this human to help her, she was bound by the forest to help him in return. She had to treat it as a trade.

If she didn't let him help her, she would be trapped here. Finally, she craned her neck and snatched the rope in her jaws. The boy pulled with surprising strength. She tried to assist by pushing herself up the wall, but the stone was slick beneath her paws and she struggled to gain footing. Her teeth strained against the rope and at last she let go, tumbling to the bottom again.

"I'm sorry!" the boy said with a gasp. He disappeared again, and scuffling sounded overhead before he reappeared, lowering himself down the rope, his boots firm against the rock wall.

He landed beside her gracefully, his feet only stirring a little dust as they touched the ground. Though young, the boy was of a strong build, clearly having worked as a farmer or blacksmith, perhaps. He crouched, putting a cautious hand toward her.

"I won't hurt you," he said, speaking slowly, as though he thought she couldn't understand his words but wanted to bring comfort anyway. "If you can trust me, I will help lift you out." When Baba Yaga made no move to snap or attack, he reached out with the rope, tying the end around her

stomach. Then he climbed, his human fingers gripping the rope and his feet balancing on narrow recesses in the wall.

He leapt over the ledge and disappeared from view. A tug pulled Baba Yaga toward the wall, and then slowly the rope began to lift her up. She pushed her paws against the stone wall in an attempt to leap higher—the rope was uncomfortable around her middle even though the boy pulled at it smoothly. At last, between her maneuvering and his pulling, her head popped through the hole in the forest floor. She blinked in the light.

The boy smiled down at her. "It's okay, you're okay now." He reached down and untied the rope from around her middle. "I'm Ivan," he said.

Baba Yaga could smell the blood pumping through him. This was him. The one she'd been looking for.

CHAPTER 26

The sight of the witch made Nadya's insides feel hollow. The gray teeth protruding from her leathery gums looked like they feasted on little girls for breakfast. The eyes shone like twin moons in a starless sky, bright yet threatening.

Nadya had been foolish to come here.

"What do you seek?" the witch croaked, leaning on her cane.

Nadya stepped a foot back. Perhaps if she ran away now, Baba Yaga would be too surprised to give chase. But as she moved, a toe wiggled on one of the giant chicken feet holding up the house. She'd never be able to outrun the cottage, with its long, wiry chicken legs.

She would have to see this through.

Nadya planted her feet on the ground and tried to look the witch in the eyes, unblinking. "The tsar is getting married to my friend Katerina . . . ," she began.

Confusion crossed Baba Yaga's face, but her features soon returned to their fearsome scowl. "Continue," she said.

"If I give the tsar a wedding gift that is special enough, he'll have to offer something to me in return. The thing I'd request would be to move to the castle and live with them like . . . like a family."

Understanding seemed to flash across Baba Yaga's eyes. She stepped away from the door and beckoned Nadya forward. "Come in," she said, her voice the croak of an old frog.

Nadya hesitated. Was this how children were lured into Baba Yaga's oven?

"I won't bite," said Baba Yaga with a chuckle.

Maybe the witch wanted to swallow her whole.

"You won't eat me at all?"

Baba Yaga shook her head. "I don't want to trick you." There was a burning in her purple-flecked eyes. "*I'm* not like that."

Nadya made her way up the steps. Heat and earthy scents encased her as she entered the small cottage. So many knickknacks and trinkets covered every surface that the room dazzled with color and chaos.

As she entered, Baba Yaga gestured to the shelves and

shelves of scattered objects behind her. "Is there anything here that you could give as a gift?" she said.

Hope and relief swarmed Nadya, making her heart hum. "You mean it? I can take something?"

Baba Yaga nodded.

"And what do I give you as a trade?" Nadya asked. Terrible mistake for her to forget . . . Baba Yaga was sure to follow the old forest traditions just like the tsar did. And she had brought nothing to offer, not even her terrible sewing or one of her grainy cakes.

The question seemed to take Baba Yaga by surprise. "I

have no wish to trade," she said. The wrinkles in the old witch's face arranged themselves into a thoughtful expression as she moved to sit in a chair at the table.

This witch didn't seem at all like the villagers had described. It was as if she genuinely wanted to help.

Maybe it was a trick, and Baba Yaga would demand her trade when it was too late to refuse. Nadya would have to find a way to offer something in exchange.

The many objects on the shelves beckoned to her. There was bound to be something here to win over the tsar. Nadya hopped to the first shelf, her fingers tingling with curiosity as she lifted small vials filled with bubbling sunset-colored liquid, dried mushrooms and poisonous nightshade, a skull that looked far too human for comfort. At last, she lifted a dagger, heavy with gold and jewels.

Where had all these things come from? It seemed too much for one person. She glanced around the room. There was only a small bed in the corner. "Do you live here alone?" she asked.

"There's the raven," said Baba Yaga, though she didn't seemed too pleased to be talking about him. Then a cloud passed over the witch's face. "I have a family. But I am separated from them."

The words pricked Nadya, like a sliver under her skin, a memory long-forgotten that still itched and stung.

"Do you miss them?" she asked.

"Always," said the witch.

Nadya thought of how Katerina's songs had been a comfort when she was very little. Maybe she could comfort Baba Yaga. But no, Katerina had said she wouldn't be allowed to visit the forest from the castle.

They fell into silence. Nadya looked at the dagger, twisting it to inspect it more closely. The handle appeared to be made of bone. She gave a small shudder and started to put it back, but the rubies were so beautiful, glittering and dancing brighter than the flames in Baba Yaga's fire.

"You spoke of the tsar," the witch said into the silence. "I've heard of him . . . but I don't understand. What is he?"

Nadya was so surprised by the question that she nearly dropped the dagger. Surely, Baba Yaga knew everything? How could she not know who the tsar was?

"He rules over our village and the forest. He became the tsar when his father died during the summer," she said. "The old tsar and tsaritsa never set foot in our village, but Tsar Aleksander was visiting every few weeks. And then he asked Katerina to marry him. It was the most exciting news."

Baba Yaga's brow furrowed, as if she was struggling to follow the story.

It reminded Nadya of a time when Katerina was helping an old woman in the village relearn to weave. The woman's illness made movements and memories difficult, and both her mind and her fingers struggled to grip the threads of Katerina's explanation. But Katerina was tender and patient, carefully answering the woman's questions. Nadya could do the same.

She continued. "They're to be married at sunrise after the full moon, and then there will be a hunt—the biggest the forest has ever seen. They invited me to join them that day, but . . ." Nadya paused. Baba Yaga's face had gone pale. What had she said? If she'd angered the witch, would she be in danger?

After a horrible silence Baba Yaga finally croaked, "What hunt?"

"The tsar has called a great hunt of all the beasts— wolves, foxes, bears—of the forest." She swallowed and continued. "He says it will end with a fire to burn the forest away from the castle."

The look of fear in Baba Yaga's eyes made Nadya feel sick. Of course a hunt would be frightening to the witch. She lived in the forest just as the animals did.

"What can be done to stop it?" Baba Yaga asked, her voice suddenly shaking.

She'd always heard of the witch as someone to be afraid of, someone threatening. Nadya had never considered that the witch could feel threatened. That her power and magic weren't enough to make her feel safe.

And suddenly Nadya knew what trade she could offer Baba Yaga in exchange for the dagger to give to the tsar.

She had never liked Tsar Aleksander's plan, his boasts of conquering the forest with fire. If she could find a way to stop it, to convince Katerina that Tsar Aleksander shouldn't burn the forest, then it was a trade worth making.

CHAPTER 27

*Z*ima clenched the cane in her bony hand. She had to stop the tsar before it was too late. She needed to *do* something, or this hunt could destroy her entire pack.

When their parents died, Grom had stepped up as the leader. If there were fights or challenges or threats, he made the decisions about what to do.

But she couldn't go to Grom. He wouldn't trust the news coming from Baba Yaga. He wouldn't believe that she was really Zima. And word of the hunt coming from the very human that Zima was supposed to have killed would make everything worse.

She ached with longing for Grom's strength, Leto's

nerve, Potok's watchfulness. For the first time, deciding how to protect her pack fell solely on Zima.

She was breathless. A heavy lump in her throat made it difficult to swallow.

Nadya was peering out the window, as though she could see hunters approaching. The dagger glittered in the light from the fireplace as she twisted it in her hands. "I am going to the castle . . . ," she said, turning back to Zima. Her hands were steady and she squared her shoulders. "Let me try to stop the hunt."

Let the girl stop the hunt? No, Zima couldn't do that. And she couldn't leave the protection of her pack to someone else—to a human. Grom would never forgive her.

"No," said Zima, "I must act." She tried to stand, but her legs were shaking. She could feel the fear pulsing inside her. She had managed to go to the witch to save Leto, and she'd stared down a single hunter. But this was too much. An entire pack of humans was going to have the greatest hunt the forest had ever seen. How could she, a solitary wolf trapped in a witch's body, ever hope to stop something so dangerous? She didn't know if she had the strength to do it.

"You can't stop them," said Nadya. "Katerina is too afraid of you—she says the forest curses everything it touches. But if I tell her how you've helped me, she'll have to understand." Nadya clutched the dagger close to her chest. "Let me. This will be my trade. I do this for you in exchange for this gift that you have given me."

For a moment Zima realized how vulnerable she was, alone with a human holding a weapon. The smell of Leto's blood, oozing from the gash made by a human knife, filled her memory. She couldn't let the hunt put him in danger again.

She eyed the dagger in the girl's hands. The girl wasn't threatening her. The dagger wasn't a weapon; it was something else.

She remembered the moment when she had chosen not to kill Nadya. Nadya hadn't tried to attack Zima, hadn't put up a fight. That moment had created a bond between them. Zima realized that she did trust this human girl. She couldn't say why, but she did.

"We just have to find the castle," said Nadya. "I know it's along that road somewhere. And Tsar Aleksander said it was near the edge of the forest."

In that, maybe Zima could do something. Before, when Leto had started to attack "Baba Yaga," she'd raised her eyes to the ceiling and shouted "Help!" and the house . . . helped. It had taken her away to another part of the forest.

She looked up. Maybe she could ask the hut for help again. The raven had said she just needed to ask nicely.

"Please . . . house"—she gripped the table, as her legs were still wobbling nervously—"please take us to the castle."

For several seconds there was silence. Zima's ears were ringing. She began to wonder if she'd merely imagined talking out loud but hadn't actually said anything. She opened her mouth to speak again when the floor beneath her feet gave a shudder. A thundering footstep sounded from under the hut as the first chicken leg took a step, and then the house took off with the speed and force of a shooting star.

The walls thumped and bumped. The floor beneath her feet swayed. Zima sat in one of the chairs, hoping it would make the light-headed feeling go away.

Nadya looked a lot better than Zima felt. She gazed at the floor in wonder, as though trying to see the galloping chicken legs through cracks in the wooden boards. "We're really going to the castle?"

Zima wanted to nod, but her head still felt dizzy. "Should be," she croaked.

Nadia tugged a paper from her bag and examined it. "This will be the farthest in the forest I've ever been." Then a smile lit her face. "Don't worry," she said. "Katerina . . . is my friend. She might fear you, but she'll listen to me."

The hut slowed to a stop and lowered to the ground, but Zima's stomach kept heaving as though the chicken legs were still stomping through the forest. She peered through the window, but the surrounding trees told her nothing—they could have been any trees in any part of the forest. She missed the wolf nose that would have allowed her to smell the differences, how the magpies and butterflies compared to the ones near the home place, and whether humans or other wolves had been through the area in the past few hours.

The door protested as Nadya opened it, but Zima stepped with the human girl across the threshold.

If the hut did what she asked, then they were somewhere near the castle. Now, what exactly a castle was, she wasn't sure. Zima squeezed the top of her cane and hoped Nadya would know it when she saw it.

The trees in the distance were thinner, younger. A faint glint of silvery light winked from beyond the saplings. Not the yellow-white of normal sunshine, this light was colder, like the light that bounces off snow.

As they shuffled toward the light, a colossal form started to take shape.

There was a meadow just beyond the trees, and it rolled like a soft cloud up to a white wall, taller than the tallest trees nearby, but nothing compared to the structure that rose behind it. Pure white towers jutted into the sky like icicles growing from the ground. The blue onion-shaped roofs were the only way to see where the towers ended and the clouds began. And everywhere—from windows, the points of the roofs, and the gates in the wall—there was the glint of gold.

This was a mountain. Zima stared in wonder. How could humans possibly build something so large, more beautiful and sparkling than the sun?

Leaves crunched as Nadya took a few steps forward, clutching the dagger, which she'd wrapped in a thin and ragged cloth. The bright light before them illuminated her eager face. "They won't want me returning to the forest," she said. "But I'll try to sneak out and visit you. I'll come to you by sundown, so you'll know when you're safe from the hunt. And you won't be alone." With that, she stepped forward to cross the meadow.

Zima longed to follow but held back, watching as Nadya joined other humans on the road approaching the castle.

As she returned to the hut, shame pulsed inside her like a second heartbeat. She had thought going to Baba Yaga to save Leto was proof that she could do what was necessary to protect her family. But now here she was, desperately searching for the courage inside her to face the human hunters herself, and unable to find it.

When it came to being a leader for her family, she wasn't strong enough.

CHAPTER 28

Baba Yaga was almost jittery with excitement, as though she were a young witch again. Here was the one she'd been looking for. A little younger and less fearsome than she'd hoped, perhaps, but she could smell the old tsar's blood in him. This young man would surely want to reclaim his tsardom, and Baba Yaga could return to her quiet solitude in peace.

Ivan was diligent in checking that she had no injuries from her fall. As soon as he was satisfied, he stood, ready to continue on his journey. Baba Yaga took a deep breath. What she was about to say would give him a shock. Humans knew that magic occurred in the forest, but meeting a talking wolf was likely to be strange for anyone.

She gave a low bow, and began, *Thank you for saving me, young man,* in as eloquent a voice as she could muster. In situations such as these, one was bound by the traditions of the forest. Ivan had saved her, and this meant that she owed him a favor in return. She only hoped it would not take too long.

As expected, Ivan gave a yelp, his light eyes wide with surprise.

My apologies for frightening you, she said, *but I must thank you for saving me. It is my duty now to return the favor.*

"You can talk?" said Ivan.

Baba Yaga frowned. Was he going to waste time like this? *Yes, yes, I can talk. Within the forest, its magic gives me that power. Outside of it, I remain an ordinary wolf.*

He raised a skeptical brow. "And you said you owe me?" said Ivan.

Yes, I am bound by the rules of this forest to trade favor for favor, spell for spell, gift for gift. In saving me, you are owed a favor as a reward. Name what you wish, and I will do it.

Ivan watched her for a moment, thinking. Then he began to pace, his heavy steps stirring up the dust of the road, his pack jangling. Baba Yaga trotted along beside him.

She had avoided humans for so many years, refusing to think of the man who had been murdered while regret ate away at her little by little. But now all of that would be set right. He was the one, the descendant of the tsar who had been murdered all those years ago.

There was so little time, only a few days left until the full moon. She hoped the favor he requested could be done swiftly. But whatever it was, it was worth doing if it earned his trust. He needed to believe her, to accept that he was the true tsar. It would almost certainly come as a shock. She would reveal the truth to him slowly, until he would have no choice but to accept the responsibility of taking back his throne.

Ivan was muttering to himself now. Baba Yaga crept closer.

"Baba Yaga," he said.

She caught the words, but wondered if she'd imagined them.

What did you say? she asked breathlessly.

"Baba Yaga," he repeated. He ran a nervous hand through his straw-colored hair. "My grandmother used to tell a story about how our family lost its home many years ago. It was the fault of the witch Baba Yaga." He heaved a sigh that was filled with regret, not his own, but passed down through generations. His grandmother's resentment lived on in him. "I love the home I grew up in here on the edge of the forest, but my grandmother could never forgive the witch for taking our old home away. She wanted to punish Baba Yaga, to seek vengeance for destroying what was ours."

He began to pace again, nervously twisting a ring on his finger. His loping steps indicated that he had grown taller only recently, and he hadn't yet gotten used to the movement. Baba Yaga glanced at her own legs and tail, so new to her as well, masking the witch inside. Despite appearances, Ivan was just a boy.

"Where did you get that ring?" asked Baba Yaga.

He looked down at the large ruby sparkling against his hand. "My grandmother gave it to me. She used to say she'd tell me one day where it came from." A dark cloud passed over his face, and he continued, "She died three days ago. It's why I left my home—I'm going to the city in the south to help my family." He shuddered, though from sadness or fear it was hard to be sure. "But I'd rather not—I want to do what my grandmother couldn't. I wish to go to Baba Yaga."

And what will you do when you meet her? said Baba Yaga, careful to keep her tone smooth and disinterested.

"I don't know," said Ivan. "My grandmother was a strong woman, much stronger than me." He paused, his eyes heavy with sadness and admiration. "She didn't just want our home back, she wanted revenge against the witch for taking what was ours."

And is this what you wish to do? said Baba Yaga.

"I don't know," he said again. He took a few uncertain steps down the road, as though he might go to the city after all. "I want to honor my grandmother. But I don't want to hurt anyone. I don't know what I'll do," he repeated. "But I need to face her."

Baba Yaga let out the breath that she'd been holding. A plan had begun to form in her mind. *I can take you to the witch's home, the house on chicken legs. I cannot deliver her to you.*

"How do I know I can trust you?" said Ivan, continuing to walk along the road.

You do not, said Baba Yaga. *You must choose to trust.*

Ivan stopped walking. They had reached a fork in the road. To the left, the road departed the forest, leading toward the city. To the right was a path that wound around the forest's edge toward the castle.

He stared at the junction as though his two choices were spread out before him. He looked back the way he had come. "My mama wants me to go to the city to seek my fortune. I wish I could stay and live by the forest—I don't want to leave."

Is that what you want, to explore the forest? said Baba Yaga. *If you come with me, you will have it, and the home your grandmother longed for, and the fortune your mama desires.* She turned toward the trees, beckoning him to follow her. *Your choice is not between your home and the city. There is always a third choice, for those brave enough to seek it.*

Ivan stared at the roads, then slowly, silently, moved his boot off the path. He observed his feet as though surprised at what he was doing. But he raised his gaze to meet hers. "I will follow you," he said. "Take me to Baba Yaga."

CHAPTER 29

ozens of families from villages Nadya had never seen or heard of stood in a line that wove toward the arched doorway to the castle, all clutching wedding gifts for the tsar and Katerina.

As the crowd moved through the entryway, guards stationed along the line snapped at people, warning them not to touch any of the painted walls or sculptures. The ceiling twinkled with floating crystals. Carvings of flowers and vines flowed down the walls, waterfalls of beauty and color. Nadya had never seen anything like it. It was hard to believe that Katerina now lived in a place like this.

The thrill of her having met Baba Yaga, and the anxiety about how she would be received now that she was at the castle, swirled together in her stomach. She tightened her grip on the dagger. She could feel the hard bone and metal through the thin cloth.

At long last, she entered a receiving room. Courtiers in furs and glittering gowns lined the walls, moving with such grace that Nadya almost wished she were invisible. Katerina could play the part of a tsaritsa, but everyone would recognize Nadya for what she was in an instant—an orphan from the edge of the forest, with no family and no home.

The line moved, and the far wall came into view. At the foot of an enormous tapestry stood two silver thrones. On one sat the tsar in black furs with red jewels glittering on his fingers.

The other throne was empty.

Nadya clutched the dagger even tighter, its rubies digging into her palm. Where was Katerina?

When it was her turn, she bowed and looked up at the tsar.

He wore a bored expression as he stared out across the room—almost as if he didn't see the mass of people assembled before him. A goblet was handed to him by a servant and he swirled it before taking a delicate sip. Scarlet droplets clung to his beard. He sniffed before turning to her.

Nadya waited for recognition but it did not come.

"Excuse me, your illustrious highness, but where is Katerina?" she said. She fought to keep the shaking from her voice. The tsar knew her; he had to be delighted to see her.

His eyes narrowed as if he was trying to remember, then at last they brightened.

"Ah, Nadya, you have come to us," he said. His voice was dry and crisp, as though it might snap.

An icy feeling crawled down Nadya's spine. The tsar had not been exactly friendly to her before, but he'd never been so cold. His power and authority filled the room, so strong she could almost smell it. All traces of warmth were gone.

"Yes, your illustrious highness," said Nadya, giving another bow and doing her best to play the part of someone at home among the splendor. "I have brought your wedding gift, but I also came in the hopes of accepting Katerina's offer to stay with you." It was a bold thing to say, pretending as though he'd already confirmed she could stay, but Katerina was not there to correct her, nor Mrs. Orlova to give her assessment.

The tsar's lips twitched. "I am afraid my dear Katerina is ill, and unable to receive visitors," he said, as though the words meant nothing.

But comprehension tightened around Nadya's neck like a snake. Katerina unwell? Nadya had never seen Katerina have so much as a sniffle. "I am an excellent healer," she said, which was a stretch but had a crumb of truth. She had helped Katerina bandage the broken arm of a girl in the orphanage once. "May I see her, your illustrious highness?" Nerves made the words twist on her tongue.

"You have brought us a wedding gift," said the tsar, ignoring her question. "I am eager to see what you have brought."

Nadya looked down. The hilt of the dagger peeked from its cloth wrapper, and a ruby glinted in the dim light. She shifted the bundle in her arms to hide it.

"It is my wish to present it to both you *and* Katerina," she said.

The tsar stiffened.

Nadya felt her knees weaken. She had gone too far. No one would dare to deny the tsar his demand.

The tips of his fingers tightened around the stem of his goblet. "Of course," he said. "You are eager to see your friend. And I would not deny her the pleasure of your visit.

Anything for my beloved." Nadya didn't like how he said the word "beloved."

He snapped his fingers and a guard appeared at his side. The guard's blue-and-white tunic was trimmed with gold and draped down his short legs to his knees. Eyeglasses perched on the guard's broad nose. "Izel, take this young lady to see Katerina."

Confusion crossed the guard's face, though he clearly dared not contradict his master.

The tsar waved a hand, gesturing for Nadya to follow the guard. As she stepped closer, the tsar's voice slithered toward her, low enough that only she could hear. "You might find her quite altered, since you last saw her." Nadya recognized in his face a hint of worry. "It is my greatest hope that she will not be unwell for our wedding. Perhaps a visit from you will revive her," he said.

Maybe it was his fears that made him so altered. If Nadya could help heal Katerina, everything would be as it should.

With that whispered wish, he dismissed her.

"Excuse me!" said Nadya, trotting to keep up with the guard as he took quick, purposeful steps down the long and twisting corridor.

"Yes?" he said, turning to her. Nadya felt like she could trust the expression in his dark eyes. His kind face, with the bronze cheeks of a man from the southern plains, was surrounded by straight black hair.

"What did the tsar mean that Katerina is ill? What's wrong with her?"

"I wish I could tell you, young mistress," he said. He removed his eyeglasses and wiped them with a handkerchief. "She's not been well ever since she arrived. There's been no word from any of the castle healers as to what's ailing her. I am surprised that he's allowing you to see her."

"What do you mean?" Her cheeks warmed with sudden worry.

The guard stopped. He tugged on his uniform to straighten it. "No one else has been permitted to approach her rooms. We soldiers have taken shifts guarding the door, to prevent anyone from entering."

Heartache stabbed Nadya, sharper than the dagger in her hands. Katerina, locked away, ill, with no one to see or comfort her. Well, Nadya was here now. She was grateful to the tsar for letting her visit Katerina.

Izel marched Nadya past two guards stationed at a final door. With a nod to one of them, he turned the handle and allowed Nadya to slip past him inside.

The room could have held the entire orphanage, including the chicken coop in the yard. Ceilings soared overhead in great swooping arches. Nadya had never cared much for weaving or sewing, but she couldn't help admiring the lush fabrics upholstering the furniture and draped around the large bed in the corner.

The guard stooped to speak to her in a low voice. "I hope that you give her strength."

As quietly as she could, Nadya approached the bed. "Katerina?" she said cautiously. "Katerina, are you awake?"

"Nadya?" said a voice. "Is that you?"

The words were hardly a whisper, as though Katerina's once-musical voice had waned to only a trace of itself.

Nadya quietly leaned in. The face that greeted her was barely recognizable. It seemed wilted, the once-full lips and cheeks now sunken and worn.

Nadya fought against the twisting of her insides, the

demon that dared to whisper that Katerina—perfect, unstoppable Katerina—was dying.

"Oh . . . Katerina . . . ," said Nadya. She wanted to throw her arms around her, but was afraid that the force of it might crush her. So instead, she patted Katerina on the arm. "I am glad to see you."

"I've missed you too," said Katerina.

In that moment all memories of the promise Nadya had made to Baba Yaga were forgotten, so consumed was she with worry and concern for her friend.

CHAPTER 30

The sun had set, and still Zima had seen no sign of Nadya. The girl had said she would return. What if something had happened to her? Or worse, what if she had lied, and it was never her intention to help stop the hunt?

The second thought sprouted a seed of fear. It twisted and tangled like a weed. The girl had seemed like she was telling the truth, but she was still a human. Grom always said that lies came naturally to humans.

Nothing good had come from Zima's interactions with humans. First Grom had punished her for sparing Nadya's life, and then the hunter had stabbed Leto. Baba Yaga herself had even told Zima not to speak to any humans, and Zima hadn't listened.

You let your fears control you, Grom had told her once, and that's exactly what Zima had done by sending Nadya to the castle while she stayed in the hut.

She had to do something. She couldn't let fear stand in her way any longer.

But what could she do? Nadya had said that no one would listen to Baba Yaga, that Katerina was too afraid of her.

For a moment Zima remembered how she'd pretended to be frightening to Veter. She'd convinced him to seek safety by pretending she was going to curse him. She could do the same for Katerina. She could pretend that she truly was the dangerous witch Baba Yaga. Maybe if she pretended to be fearless, it would almost start to feel like she was.

She swallowed. She wouldn't let fear control her.

Come morning, she would go to the castle and talk to Katerina herself.

The raven still had not returned by the time she woke, but Zima was glad he was gone. She didn't need him telling her what a dangerous plan this was, or that it was in violation of Baba Yaga's instructions. She'd already broken the rules by moving the hut and speaking to Nadya, so she would just have to bear the witch's wrath if she ever returned.

Her cane thudded against the soft wood as she descended the steps. The crackling sound of the leaves beneath her feet put her on edge. When she reached the ground, the hut pulled up its steps and retreated into the shadows, its chicken legs tiptoeing to avoid footprints. She could just see its windows, glittering like eyes in the darkness, but the fanned branches of fir trees shielded it from the view of those who didn't know where to look.

A road snaked toward the castle gate. It wouldn't take long to get there from her place on the edge of the forest. The gate was closed, as it was early morning, and the road not yet bustling with humans taking their wedding gifts to the tsar. The time to go was now.

She took a deep breath. Her body wanted to feel scared. It wanted to shiver and twitch, to retreat to the safety of the hut. For the first time in her life, she would approach the humans by choice.

Did Baba Yaga feel this scared when she left her hut? Zima tried to imagine herself as a formidable witch, capable of cursing anyone who dared stand in her way. Katerina would end the hunt because she demanded it.

Zima moved to the road and followed it to the gate. The castle seemed to grow taller as she drew nearer, until it blocked the sun and the sky entirely. There was nothing else in the world but this giant place, and the people inside who had the power to save or destroy everything in the world that mattered to Zima.

The gold bars of the gate formed an emblem of two

eagles, each with one wing outstretched. It looked familiar, though Zima couldn't say from where.

A human was visible through the bars. Zima took a breath. She was Baba Yaga, feared throughout the forest.

"Hold, Grandmother!" boomed a voice. "If you are bringing a wedding gift for his illustrious highness, the gates will open at midday."

A man watched her from just behind the gate. He was stout with a round trunk-like chest. Balanced on his nose were two pieces of glass, like the windows in Baba Yaga's hut, held up by golden wires. They enlarged his eyes, giving him the look of an insect.

"What business do you have here?" the man demanded.

With a final steadying breath, Zima said, "I am Baba Yaga." She tried to sound as threatening as possible, but her voice came out as a croak. She coughed to clear her throat. "And I am here to see Katerina."

The man's jaw slackened. "You're—you're . . . ," he stammered, and Zima couldn't tell if it was in fear or surprise. Then in a low voice he said, "You're Baba Yaga?" He held up his hands in submission. "Please, don't hurt me."

Zima nodded. "If you take me to Katerina, I shall not harm you. Now let me in!" She tried to remember how Baba Yaga had looked and sounded in her most intimidating moments, and extended a crooked finger at the guard. It was *almost* threatening.

It worked. With trembling hands the man pulled out what looked to be a set of metal twigs on a metal ring. "You won't curse me?" he asked, one of the metal twigs pinched between his fingers.

"Not if you do as I ask and let me inside," she said, her confidence swelling a little.

The man nodded, and he shoved the metal twig into a contraption on the gate, then turned it. It clicked, and the gate swung open. "We will need to be quick and go through the servants' wing. I will explain why inside." He watched her in a sort of fearful excitement. "You will want to cover your face as best you can," he said, pointing at the cloth wrapped about Zima's neck and shoulders. He helped her to tug it over her hair and around her mouth.

Zima was almost as surprised as he appeared to be. She was going to see Katerina! This was going better than she could have hoped.

Through the gate she found herself in a cluster of low buildings. People scurried around, hauling sacks and pulling carts stacked high with wood. It was busier even than the village had been on the day Leto was injured, with people crowding the paths, their eyes narrowed with concentration.

Once or twice another guard marched past, and each time Zima's guard steered her in a different direction. Zima was too pleased at her good fortune in being taken to Katerina to worry.

But as the path turned, Zima stopped still, breathless.

Row after row of animal pelts were hung up to dry in the sun. The skins were stretched across wooden beams, a faint breeze rippling through the fur.

The full weight of her mission pressed on Zima. This was a horrible place, a deadly place. For a moment she thought she might be sick. But the guard urged her to follow him quickly, and she tore her eyes away from the disgusting sight.

It was then that Zima remembered where she'd seen the image on the gate. It was on the side of the fancy cart she'd seen in the village. The woman she had seen in the cart must have been Katerina on her way to the castle.

The guard led her through the grounds toward the largest of the buildings, the one with blue rooftops that stretched into the sky. A wooden door on the side of the building creaked as the guard swung it open.

Darkness hung in the corridor like fog. It was almost impossible to see where the hall turned, but the guard kept a tight grip on her elbow. Zima leaned heavily on her cane. Once or twice she tripped in the darkness, but both guard and cane kept her from tumbling to the ground. Their footsteps echoed in the narrow hall.

He led her through another door and then down a few steps. Somehow this corridor was even darker than the first. It was strange how the walls could shine such a bright white on the outside while the inside was dark as a cave.

A damp passage led to a set of stairs. The guard waited on the bottom step, his ragged breathing filling the small space. He motioned for her to follow, and together they climbed, Zima's joints aching as she pushed herself up step after step.

Each time voices sounded ahead, the guard led Zima away from them, down another passage. Twice they doubled back the way they had come. After an age of twisting down narrow corridors, he opened a door and they entered a plain room with a long wooden table and a dozen chairs tucked under each side. The plain white walls and polished tabletop glistened like the surface of a frozen lake.

At last, the man relaxed. He stumbled to a chair at the end of the table and sank into it, his feet hovering a little off the floor. Sweat beaded at his temples where his black hair stuck to his golden skin. A chair stood empty opposite him, and Zima sat down.

He stared at Zima through the glass pieces perched on his nose, with narrowed eyes as though trying to track some elusive prey.

"They said you would come," he said. "I was supposed to bring anyone matching your description directly to the tsar. But I have not. I think I know why you're here, and I want to help you." His dark eyes brimmed with nervous anticipation. His round face was hopeful. "My name is Izel."

Zima tried to bury her surprise. She was expected. But before she could think of what to say, Izel continued. "They say that when the tsar's great-grandfather took power many years ago, he declared that no one should dare defy him, because he had the powers of Baba Yaga on his side." His pudgy lips formed a frown. "A select few of us believe his story was a lie. That he took over the castle in defiance of you, not with your help. We hoped that you would come to curse him for using your name. After so many years, most lost hope." His frown shifted into a smile as he whispered conspiratorially, "And now, you are here."

Her confusion must have shown on her face because his brows knitted, and he leaned forward to say, "Is this why you have come? Are you here to curse the tsar?"

If she had been in her wolf body, her fur would have stood on end. No, that wasn't why she was here at all. She needed to be taken to Katerina.

She opened her mouth to correct Izel but shut it again. She couldn't appear nervous. He had to believe that her search for Katerina was all part of a plan to curse the tsar. Then he might help her.

"Why do you wish me to curse the tsar?" she asked, trying to use the same prodding voice that Baba Yaga had once used with Zima.

Izel looked around the room, as though he expected the tsar to be perched on the wall like a spider to listen to their conversation. "The tsar is a monster."

The words unbalanced Zima. She knew the tsar was a threat because he planned the hunt and the fire. But she hadn't expected the humans to think him horrible too.

"Ever since he inherited the throne," Izel continued, "he has threatened violence to those serving him. My wife—" He stopped, his breath catching in his throat. "She wakes up in the middle of the night, screaming from dreams where I am thrown into the dungeons or beaten. I would do anything to make her fears go away, even if it means disobeying orders."

Anxiety trickled down the back of Zima's neck but

she couldn't let it show. Izel needed to believe in her. She hunched her shoulders and tried to arrange her face into a most frightening scowl. "I need to speak with Katerina," she said. "It is all part of my plan."

Confusion flashed across Izel's face, but he recovered quickly. "Of course," he said. "But with the tsar and other guards looking for you, we must be careful. I am afraid Katerina has been very ill. Only those close to her have been allowed to see her, and guards are stationed at her door." He added, "Though I suppose your magic could take care of them."

"I can't do—" Zima stopped herself and swallowed. Coming to the castle was like prodding her nose into a hornet's nest. She couldn't keep threatening curses if a curse was what they *wanted*. "No, I should not. No one can know I am here."

Izel pressed a finger on his chin, thinking. "We can hide you here in the castle until I can find a way to take you to Katerina without anyone seeing." He thought for another moment before smiling. "I have an idea. The kitchens. We can pretend you're a new servant here to help with preparations for the wedding." The corners of his mouth twitched. "You'd be as concealed as I can keep you from the tsar. He never enters the kitchens." Standing from his own chair, Izel reached out an arm to assist Zima to her feet. "The cook Lubov frightens him."

He led her down a short, plain corridor. Through an open

door came strong smells of roasted meat. Two women were visible, one brandishing a large silver knife. She was tall, with deep lines creasing her pink forehead and skin hanging from her jaw like a rooster's waddle. Her face contorted in fury and she held the knife above her head, looking ready to hurl it at the girl facing her. This must be Lubov.

Zima looked back at Izel and saw him waiting for her answer. How could she possibly pretend to be human for so many hours among so many people? She had no idea what humans did in a kitchen. She'd be of no use and then the angry woman would threaten her with the knife.

But she stood a better chance of convincing people she was human than she did of performing magic. Zima gritted her teeth. "Okay," she said, "I'll do it."

Izel's eyes sparkled. "She'll be glad for your assistance, so long as she doesn't find out who you are. But you look no different from any other old woman, though perhaps a *bit* older than most." He eyed the many wrinkles that gave her hands the look of tree bark. "What shall we call you?" he asked.

Call her? The only human names she knew were Nadya and Katerina.

"How about Galina?" Izel suggested.

Zima practiced saying the name. *Galina. Galina.* Yes, she could answer to that name.

Blasts of hot air and smoke blew through the kitchen

door. The cook Lubov was still shouting. Zima winced at the sharp words. But an angry cook was nothing if it meant Zima could stop the hunt. And she'd only have to keep up the act until she found Katerina.

Just before they went through the door, Izel gripped her shoulder and said with an expression of utmost seriousness, "If you don't wish to be caught, you must stay in the kitchens until my signal. If you go wandering about, Tsar Aleksander will certainly find you."

CHAPTER 31

Katerina woke with a gasp, gulping in air. She threw her arms in front of her face as though shielding herself.

Nadya nearly fell out of her soft chair by the window. She hadn't realized she'd been half-asleep, but her hand tingled where she'd been leaning on it.

Grabbing a cloth, Nadya rushed to Katerina's side and began dabbing at the sweat trickling down her forehead and cheeks. "It's okay," she said, trying to mimic the warm voice she'd heard Mrs. Orlova use when caring for the younger girls. Nadya herself had been feverish a few winters ago, and Mrs. Orlova and Katerina had stayed by her side, offering her spoonfuls of broth, warm and tart, washing her face as

Nadya was doing now. Nadya couldn't manage the soothing tones like they could, but she tried. "You're awake now, in the castle."

"She's going to take me!" Katerina whimpered, not yet opening her eyes.

"No one will take you. I'm here," said Nadya.

Katerina's wide eyes fluttered open and she blinked, glancing about as though not believing where she was.

Taking Katerina's wrists, Nadya gently lowered her arms so that they were no longer clutching at her face. "You're in the castle," she repeated.

"I was in the forest," Katerina said, her breath quickening again. "Baba Yaga wanted to take me. And . . . and Mrs. Orlova stopped her."

At the mention of Baba Yaga, Nadya's stomach heaved, as though its contents had curdled. Not because she believed in Katerina's dream, but because she'd been at the castle a whole day without fulfilling her promise to the witch. Yet now didn't seem like a good time to speak of Baba Yaga, not while Katerina was so distressed.

"You haven't been in the forest in many years, Katerina," she said calmly. "And besides, you're grown now. She only eats naughty children." Though no one had seemed less likely to eat a child than the Baba Yaga who Nadya had encountered. Nadya pressed flat the smile that threatened to curl her mouth.

Katerina shook her head and swallowed. "No, no, this was different. Not like when I saw—" She swallowed again, then continued, "In the dream I was much smaller. Maybe even a baby."

"Well, that's how you know it was only a dream," Nadya said. "You're here now. And Baba Yaga has no reason to come here." It wasn't all the way true, not yet, but Nadya would make it so.

CHAPTER 32

Lubov looked Zima up and down, her eyes lingering on Zima's shaking hands. "*You* want a position in *my* kitchens?" She didn't even attempt to hide her skepticism. Her eyes were bright and alert, surrounded by loose skin. She seemed to see everything going on in the busy kitchens at once, though she never took her gaze off Zima.

"You need the help," said Izel. "I've brought her to help you." His jaw jutted out and he put his hands on his hips.

Lubov looked like she was ready to argue, but instead, she huffed and shoved a broom into Zima's free hand, ordering her to sweep the floors before they got to work on supper.

Zima's stomach relaxed, if only a little. At least she knew

what a broom was, and what it was for, thanks to the raven. She brushed it against the floor. The sound reminded her of the winter wind rustling leafless twigs and branches on the trees. She hoped the raven wasn't too worried when he returned to find her gone. If she could talk to Katerina soon, maybe she could even be back at the hut before he returned.

She dragged the broom around the kitchen, brushing up whatever she could find on the floor—dust, ashes, vegetable and fruit peels. The kitchen workers clanged metal cooking instruments and thrust wooden spoons into large pots, too busy to pay her any notice. The air was thick with steam and smoke from the fires. Droplets of sweat trickled down Zima's forehead.

She couldn't help but notice that she hadn't heard the chatter of the forest voices as much since arriving at the castle. It was strange. The magical whispers were a constant flow after she switched bodies with Baba Yaga, but now they were hardly more than a dribble.

Though it was possible she simply couldn't hear the voices over the noise of the kitchens. With Lubov's constant shouting it was hard to focus on anything other than the duties to be done. Besides that night's supper, every cook was busy with preparations for the wedding feast, which they were constantly reminded was only three days away. As soon as Zima swept up the pumpkin skins and onion layers, more appeared. And Lubov hurled insults across the room as often as she gave commands, punctuating them with the thwack of her spoon against the counter. Even the clang of pans and chopping of knives couldn't drown out her orders.

Everyone was talking about the wedding. It was to be a large gathering, with many visitors from far-off places. And they were all expected to give the tsar gifts. Beyond that, Zima didn't know much. Humans had so many odd names for very specific things, it was hard to keep track.

The day was long, and it was exhausting work. Everyone in the kitchen seemed overwhelmed with the number of tasks to be done. There were six people in all besides Zima and Lubov, and each seemed to have their own special assignment. The foods were more complex than Zima could ever have imagined. She watched in wonder as they combined vegetables, meats, and herbs in a pot to form stew, or when powders and milk were placed into an oven and then emerged as a solid loaf.

The smells were so enticing they made Zima's knees weak. She hadn't had anything in days other than the raw roots in Baba Yaga's hut. But when she tried to eat some of the food being made, Lubov slapped her hand and ordered her to continue sweeping.

At last, it was the end of the day, and Lubov declared that they could sit down to their own meal. Zima's chair groaned as she sank into it. Her joints throbbed. The others around the table looked tired but not nearly as exhausted as Zima felt. They chattered happily among themselves as Lubov circled the table, dishing a bright-red soup into the bowl placed before each person.

A gurgle erupted from Zima's stomach. The steam drifted past her nose, bringing with it the scent of roots and wild onions.

As soon as the soup sloshed into Zima's bowl, she plunged into it with her mouth. Scarlet drops flecked her face as she lashed at the soup with her tongue. The tip of her nose burned from the heat of the liquid, but she ignored it. She licked until there wasn't a drop left in the bowl.

Suddenly the silence of the room pressed in on her ears. Zima raised her head. Each person at the table was staring

at her, some with their mouths hanging open, some with barely contained grins that caused their chins to tremble.

The girl sitting next to Zima let out a small cough, and Zima looked up. She recognized her as the girl in charge of all the baking. She had golden hair, the color of honey or a bread's crust, and her cheeks were always smudged with flour. The girl held up a spoon with a pointed look at Zima, dipped it into her soup, and took a sip from it.

Zima's stomach dropped. She'd already done something wrong. The humans around the table all drank their soup in the same way, by dipping the utensil in the liquid and sipping. She fought the urge to stand from the table and rush out the door. They could probably all guess that she wasn't human.

The others continued to stare at Zima as soup dripped from around her lips. The girl took a few more mouthfuls of her own soup before she snapped, "What are you all staring at? Haven't you ever been hungry after a hard day?"

The others looked among themselves, eyebrows raised, shoulders shrugging, then one by one they returned to eating their meal.

Zima watched them all through her eyelashes. Her head was bowed. She wanted to dive under the table.

The girl nudged Zima's arm with her elbow. "You'll learn," she said in a low voice, before swallowing again.

*   *   *

After supper everyone filed out of the kitchen into a dark corridor. Zima had one foot in the passage when the broom handle poked in front of her, barring her way.

She looked up into the stern scowl of Lubov, who held the broom and jabbed a thumb over her shoulder at the enormous stacks of dirty dishes piled on the tables and counters.

"Your job," Lubov said. "Get to it."

With that, Lubov shoved her way past, nearly knocking Zima into the wall.

Zima stared at the mess. What was she supposed to do?

"You'll need to get some water first," said a voice.

Her whole body ached, and Zima could only turn very slowly to see who spoke. It was the girl with the golden hair who'd sat next to her at dinner. She passed Zima and made her way toward the door that led outside, picking up a bucket from a shelf. With a tilt of her head, she said, "Come, I'll show you. It'll be too much for one person . . . much easier with help."

Much easier with help . . . like a wolf pack. It surprised Zima that sometimes humans realized this too. It had been strange being so alone in Baba Yaga's hut.

The girl showed Zima how to pump water from a spout outside, then how to heat it over the fire. Lastly, they filled a tub with the dirty dishes, heated water, and soap, then with a rough brush scrubbed the pans clean.

"You do this every night?" Zima said, wiping away the damp strands of hair that clung to her forehead.

"It's better if you clean as you go," the girl said. "That way you don't have to do them all at the end of the day."

Zima bit back the urge to say that it seemed like a lot of mess that could be avoided if humans would eat their food as a wolf did. Then again, wolves didn't get to enjoy fresh bread or heated soups. Maybe some things were worth the extra effort.

After a while, the girl began to hum as she scrubbed each dish clean. The humming was surprisingly pleasant. It filled the silence and somehow made the work feel less tedious.

"What is that?" Zima asked.

"What?" the girl said, a crease appearing between her brows.

"That sound."

"Oh," the girl said, understanding. "Does it bother you? It's a song my grandmother used to sing."

Zima shook her head. "No, it's nice. Can you do it again?"

The girl's lips parted and instead of speaking, her voice made a beautiful sound, like the call of birds at sunrise. Zima didn't know human voices could do that. The sound rose and fell, twisted and flowed with all the smoothness of a stream. And the words themselves told a story of someone unable to sleep, looking to the moon on a clear night and waiting at the window for a loved one. The meaning made

Zima's insides soft, like her bones had turned to slush. It was how she felt when she looked at the moon sometimes, wishing her parents were still at her side, wishing that Grom hadn't changed so much, wishing that her family could feel safe from the dangers of the forest and the humans and Baba Yaga.

"That was beautiful," Zima said.

But the song also planted a seed of worry inside her. There were only two nights until the full moon.

"Thank you," said the girl. She plunged her hands into the soapy water and pulled out another dish. "I'm Oksana."

"Call me Galina," said Zima.

Oksana had already been so helpful that Zima dared to ask a question that had been gnawing at the back of her mind since her arrival in the kitchen. "Do you know how I can find Katerina?"

Oksana shook her head. "She's been ill since she arrived. No one is allowed to see her. I've wondered what she's like, though, the orphan who will be a tsaritsa. I hope . . ." She paused, biting her lip. "I hate to speak ill of . . . but I do worry about her, marrying the tsar. He might crush her."

So Izel wasn't the only one who thought the tsar a monster.

They didn't talk much after that and continued washing the dishes in silence. If Izel didn't return soon, Zima would have to set about finding Katerina herself.

CHAPTER 33

atch where you step, said Baba Yaga.

Her senses were heightened now that she was responsible for not only navigating the forest herself but keeping Ivan safe. She was acutely aware of how many things there were in the forest that could kill a human.

After some time walking, they stopped to eat. Ivan took a flask from his rucksack and knelt down to fill it at a stream nearby. Baba Yaga caught him out of the corner of her eye just as he was raising the bottle to his lips.

With a growl she charged toward him, snatched the bottle in her jaws, and flung it away.

"Ah! What was that for?" said Ivan.

You fool! Baba Yaga hissed. *This is a poisonous stream. The Waters of Death flow through this forest.*

Ivan stared at her in wide-eyed confusion. "But I've drunk from forest streams before, and nothing has ever come of it."

This made Baba Yaga pause. Certain pools and streams in the forest, rare ones, were filled with the Waters of Life, which would strengthen the drinker. Perhaps this accounted for Ivan's unnatural strength.

You were lucky, she said. *But from now on, you only drink when I tell you it is safe.*

Traveling with Ivan was like trying to track a dandelion seed on the wind. When they continued on their journey, Ivan ambled behind her at a distance. She turned to watch him meander among the trees, crouching to admire some plant or mushroom.

Follow closely! said Baba Yaga. *I cannot show you the safe paths if you are always wandering behind me.*

"But there is so much to see," said Ivan. "I have never journeyed this far, to the heart of the forest. How can you be tired of its wonders?"

What wonders? said Baba Yaga, surprisingly curious to hear the answer.

"I was certain I saw a firebird just now," he said.

Even Baba Yaga herself had never seen the firebird, with

its wings of flame. Some thought it a prize, others a bad omen. Baba Yaga chose not to remind Ivan of this.

What if he had been touched by bad fortune—would he be able to defeat the tsar? Baba Yaga was growing skeptical. Ivan seemed strong enough, that was certain. He could easily match the tsar for strength, though he was still a boy. And Ivan's bloodline made him the logical choice for the task.

But was he willing to fight the tsar at all? She had hoped to find someone adept at fighting, who could believably defeat the tsar in a duel. Ivan was not that. He showed none of the ruthlessness of spirit that seemed necessary to best the tsar in combat.

Yet he was so joyfully fascinated by what he saw in the forest, and that revealed a different kind of strength.

She couldn't let herself dwell on these thoughts. She needed someone to defeat the tsar, for there was no question that she could not do it herself.

She shook away her thoughts and continued on their journey. They had to keep moving. They had only two days until the full moon and her last hope of unraveling the tsar's schemes.

Then a flash of light and movement caught Baba Yaga's eye, glowing brighter as she approached a cluster of trees. The grove was illuminated by the flicker of flames. Baba Yaga looked up. Perched in a tree was indeed a firebird. Was it following them—a bad omen for Ivan? She watched as it blinked jewel-bright eyes at her.

What is it you want? she whispered.

It was silent, though the ember-like glow of its feathers was so real she could almost hear the crackle of the fireplace in her hut. Warmth filled her, smoky and comforting as black tea, and with it came gratitude, which nestled in her stomach like a hot coal. She was grateful for the forest, its dangers and magic. For the life it had given her.

As if in answer to her thoughts, the firebird spread its wings and soared through the naked tree branches, gliding away into the night.

Baba Yaga stood watching the firebird as it drifted away, not even noticing that Ivan had come up beside her.

"What's wrong?" he said.

Baba Yaga didn't know how to tell him. She could still feel the firebird's heat on her body long after its glow disappeared from view. She was certain she would never have seen a firebird if it were not for him, and it suddenly struck her how little she knew of this forest that had so long been her home. In that moment she was grateful to be traveling with him.

CHAPTER 34

Izel finally returned the next morning. Lubov started to protest, but Izel ignored her, tugging Zima by the elbow into another room to speak to her privately.

"I am to be the guard stationed at Katerina's room," he said, smoothing out his coat sleeve and clearly pleased with his own cleverness.

"And when will that be?" Zima asked. She twisted her cane in her palm. Only one night remained until the full moon, then the hunt would start the following day right after the dawn wedding. This was taking too long.

Izel straightened his spectacles. "Tomorrow morning. Have someone show you to the great hall, and I will meet you there," he said.

Tomorrow morning. And then this would all be over. She could go back to the hut to try and find a way to become a wolf again and leave this world of humans behind.

For now, she had one night to wait until she could see Katerina. One more night of pretending.

Soon, the tsar's plans would be called off. Soon, her pack would be safe.

Soon . . . so long as nothing went wrong.

That afternoon, Oksana eyed Zima's skirts and wrinkled her nose. "You know you're provided with fresh clothes to wear, right, Galina? Just ask Toma for an unsoiled uniform." She gestured at a maid who was running lengths of cloth through a basin of water, similar to how Zima and Oksana had washed the dishes.

Zima looked down. She was wearing the same dress Baba Yaga had worn on the day they switched bodies. Dark smudges soiled the front. It was covered in wrinkles. Oksana's uniform, by contrast, had a few smudges from the work of the day but was otherwise crisp and clean and gave off a hint of lavender.

Zima had always kept her fur spotless. But as she'd discovered rather quickly, her tongue wasn't very effective at cleaning her human clothes.

She crossed her arms, her cheeks growing hot. Clean

clothes seemed to be yet another thing that set her apart from the humans and showed her to be an outsider.

Part of her wanted to ignore the suggestion. She didn't have much time left in the kitchens, so what did it matter if her dress was dirty? But she looked down at Oksana's shined shoes, compared to her own, which were scuffed and caked in mud. It surprised her to realize that she wanted to fit in.

Oksana gave her a warm smile. "I can go ask Toma, if you like," she said.

Moments later, when Zima found herself in the small bedroom where she'd slept, she held up the clean frock and stared in wonder at what Toma had called "undergarments." What were all these bits of clothing—what went on first and which strings tied around what?

She threw the frock over her head and pulled it down. But which hole was for her head and which were for her arms? She tried to remember how the old dress had draped over her. After a few wrong tries, she finally got her head through what seemed to be the right hole, and her arms through the others.

When she opened her bedroom door, Oksana waited outside, leaning against the far wall. She stood upright as Zima approached.

The girl's eyes widened, and a smile stretched across her face.

"Much better," she said. "Except that it's inside out."

Cooks hurried past, grabbing ingredients from shelves and hurling them into bowls and pots. With only today and tomorrow to prepare for the dawn wedding, they were scrambling to finish preparations.

Oksana gave Zima a wink as she grabbed a new sack of flour and carried it to her station.

Zima didn't see the peels on the floor until it was too late.

Oksana stepped on one of them, her foot slipping from under her and twisting with a sickening crunch. As she fell, her head made contact with the edge of the table, then slammed against the floor.

For an endless moment, Zima's heart stopped. She stared in horror at Oksana and realized in that second that she cared for the human girl like a member of her own pack. Oksana was a friend.

Everything swirled around her as she stood, unmoving, and then suddenly it all moved at double speed. Zima stepped forward to Oksana's side, kneeling beside her and wincing with fear at the blood trickling from a cut in Oksana's head.

Lubov immediately ordered two strong servants to carry Oksana to her room and sent a maid away to call for the healer, who lived in a small cottage on the castle grounds.

Zima was ordered to continue helping with dinner preparations, though she ached to check on Oksana. But it wasn't until after the meal was prepared and Zima had finished cleaning the dishes—on her own, she realized with another pang of heartache—that she was allowed to visit her friend.

The healer was just rising from a stool beside Oksana's bed as Zima entered the room.

"How is she?" Zima asked, her voice no more than the squeak of a mouse.

"She won't wake," said the healer. He was young, hardly older than Oksana, but the dark circles under his eyes made him appear withered. They were especially pronounced in the evening light. "I'll return soon, but in the meantime, perhaps it will help her to have a friend by her side." He closed the door behind him, careful not to make a sound.

Zima took a seat on the stool. The palm that gripped her cane was slick with sweat, but she placed her other hand on Oksana's arm. The girl's skin was cold and clammy, and her breaths were shallow.

This was all Zima's fault. She'd missed the peel that Oksana slipped on.

If only she were really Baba Yaga, maybe she could heal Oksana the way the witch had healed Leto.

But it was hopeless. She didn't know how to use magic.

She would gladly be a witch if it meant Oksana would wake up.

The voices whispered that she could be. *Heal her,* they said.

She tried to remember that moment when Baba Yaga healed Leto, but the memory was foggy. The witch had muttered something under her breath. She could remember the witch's lips forming the words *Heal him.*

Without even meaning to, Zima began to do the same. "Heal her, please, heal her," she found herself muttering, over and over.

Heal her.

Please.

Heal her.

She wasn't a witch. And she didn't know magic. But there was a weight to the words. They tingled in her throat, and her palm was warm against Oksana's skin.

The room felt too hot. And there was a buzzing in the air.

Zima almost stopped speaking in her surprise, but she forced herself to keep repeating the words.

Heal her. Please, heal her.

Something was happening.

Zima didn't know what, or how, but it was.

And then, Oksana's eyes fluttered open.

Zima nearly screamed in surprise. But instead, she

kept saying the words, over and over. Until, at last, Oksana placed her hand over Zima's.

With a grin, Oksana said, "I thought Baba Yaga only cursed people. I didn't know she could heal." She licked her dry lips and smiled.

Oksana moved to sit up, with Zima helping her. But Oksana didn't seem to need helping. She was as fit as Leto had been after Baba Yaga healed his injury.

"Thank you," said Oksana. She looked at her hands, then blurted out, "Can . . . can I hug you?"

Zima leaned back. The word sounded vaguely threatening. "What's a hug?" she asked.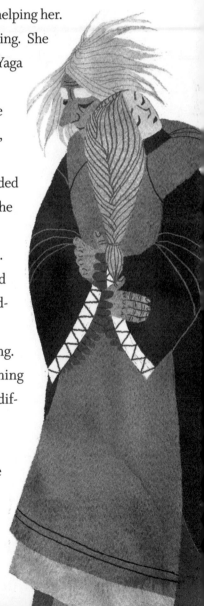

Oksana smiled at her confusion. Slowly Oksana reached forward and wrapped her arms around Zima, holding her close.

The hug was warm and comforting. Zima was used to wrestling and cleaning her brothers in her pack, but this was different. It felt peaceful and caring.

"This is a hug?" Zima asked.

Oksana pulled away. "We don't have to hug if you don't like it."

"No, it's nice," said Zima. "But what does it mean?"

"It's my way of saying thank you," said Oksana.

"Oh," said Zima. Thanking someone wasn't something they usually found time for in her pack. There were too many other dangers to worry about. She liked how Oksana had things like singing and hugging to bring joy to cold winter nights.

CHAPTER 35

aterina had improved a little in Nadya's care. Her skin was still ashen and seemed to drape over her bones, but she was able to eat and had gained the strength to stand for dress fittings and other wedding preparations. But she still needed rest, and the constant interruptions were making that impossible.

Nadya had had enough. The next person who arrived would be turned away, even if Nadya had to stand guard and force them out herself. She tugged the blankets up to Katerina's chin. The air outside was icy and the sky threatened snow.

But Katerina had been asleep barely an hour when Tsar

Aleksander burst into the room. He made no effort to quiet his footsteps or soften the slam of the door.

Nadya jumped to her feet in surprise. "Hush, your illustrious highness. Katerina only just—"

Even if the tsar had not turned white with anger, the look of horror on the faces of the guards standing behind him would have made it clear to Nadya that she had just said something very, very wrong. Only a day ago she might have been heartbroken to see that look, to realize it might ruin her chances of living in the castle.

But that didn't seem to matter anymore. Her home wasn't the castle, it was Katerina. Frustrating, caring, infuriating, loving Katerina.

"Careful," he said, a forced smile stretching his lips. "I have beaten servants for less." The disdain in his voice shocked Nadya's bones. "Leave this room. I will speak to my bride-to-be."

The words of protest were lost in Nadya's throat as a guard scooped under her arms and deposited her in the empty corridor before retreating into Katerina's room and shutting the door between them.

Nadya ground the plush carpet beneath her heel. She had grown to hate the tsar since coming to the castle. One of the maids mentioned finding the cloak Katerina wove for him among a pile of rags. This was his first time visiting Katerina in her sickness. It didn't seem as though he cared about her at all. They were supposed to be married at sunrise, and Nadya found herself wishing that she and Katerina could return to the orphanage.

The tsar's voice rattled the keyhole. "There are rumors Baba Yaga was sighted on castle grounds," he said. Something weighted his words. Was it fear?

There were steady footsteps in the room now. The tsar must have been pacing. "The witch is determined to stop this wedding. I don't yet know if she's still here, or in the forest, but she is searching for you," he said.

"She has cursed me," said Katerina. "I am certain of it." Her voice was weak and breathless. "Why else would I be so ill? I have not been the same since she came to me in the village."

The footsteps ceased. A cold dread filled Nadya. Was this true? Katerina had never said that Baba Yaga had come to her. And now, here she was, with an illness that mystified the castle healers, begun so suddenly, as soon as Katerina left the village.

No, it couldn't be true. Baba Yaga didn't seem the type to curse anyone, let alone Katerina. And she'd never even heard of Katerina or the tsar when Nadya met her in the hut. How could the witch possibly want to prevent the wedding?

The tsar seemed just as surprised as Nadya. "When did she come to you? Why didn't you tell me?"

"Because I knew she was trying to deceive me," said

Katerina, pleading. "It was before I met you. She predicted that you would fall in love with me, but she said it was because . . ." She paused.

"Because what?" said the tsar, his voice dark.

"It was lies, what she said," said Katerina. "It's why we must stop her."

"I swore to you that I would protect you from Baba Yaga, did I not, my love? My gold?" The declaration by the tsar seemed almost perfect, musical. The kind of oath a girl might swoon at, hearing it from the ruler of the tsardom. But to Nadya it sounded flat and hollow. "As long as your powers remain, you are in danger from her."

Powers?

"But if she's here, in the castle . . . ," said Katerina. "What if we delay the wedding? Just until I'm well again. Just until she's been found."

In an instant the tsar's tone turned. He let out a bark of high-pitched laughter. "My foolish girl, you have no idea what it will take to defeat the witch, even if you are of her kind."

Katerina, of Baba Yaga's kind?

Katerina, with powers?

The realization nearly knocked Nadya to her knees. She clutched at the wall. A hundred memories flooded Nadya's mind. Katerina, who could touch flowers that poisoned others. Who could heal wounds from the forest when no one else could.

Powers.

A witch.

Katerina was a witch.

"No," he said. "No, we will wed. And then my great hunt will find Baba Yaga and burn the forest. And any man, woman, or child who doesn't join . . . will be executed. I will send messengers to the village at once."

Footsteps shuddered across the floor, and the door opened so quickly that Nadya barely had time to jump back against the far wall as the tsar and his guards entered the corridor. His brow creased at the sight of her, but a forced smile stretched across his face. It did not reach his eyes.

"I am glad to see Katerina improved," he said. "Clearly, you have had a positive effect on her."

The guards moved into position beside Katerina's door once more. As Tsar Aleksander walked away, he called behind him, "Do make sure you stay within Katerina's rooms. If you leave, I *will* know."

Nadya darted inside the bedchamber and shut the door behind her, breathing hard. Executed. The tsar had just said that anyone who did not join him in hunting Baba Yaga would be executed. Everyone in the village, the other girls at the orphanage, Mrs. Orlova. Nadya felt the urge to protect them all.

Katerina was still in bed, the blankets damp with sweat. She was shivering.

The conversation Nadya had overheard echoed in her ears as she took a cautious step forward. She could barely look at Katerina. Not because of the realization that Katerina was a witch, but because Katerina hadn't said anything in protest when the tsar threatened the village. Nadya swallowed and took a breath. "The tsar said that anyone who doesn't hunt Baba Yaga will be executed." The words were sticky and hot in her mouth.

Katerina mopped her damp forehead with a handkerchief. "It is necessary. She is a threat to our village. To me."

Confusion swelled inside Nadya. How could the witch she'd met, the one who had helped Nadya without question and who had never even heard of the tsar, be a threat?

She had always admired Katerina. But in this, she was sure Katerina was wrong. The words pressed against her lips, but she held them in, afraid that if she let them out, everything would change between her and her friend.

But everything had changed. Katerina didn't live in the orphanage anymore. And she was marrying the tsar even when he didn't love her, when he was threatening everyone in Katerina's old life. If Katerina sided with the tsar in this, all friendship between her and Nadya would be broken.

She feared that even more than the tsar's threats.

"The tsar wants to execute us," Nadya repeated. "How can you agree with that?" She remembered the chill of the tsar's words. "He . . . he doesn't care that you're sick."

Katerina spluttered, her breathing quickened. "He does, he promised . . ." She hesitated, clasping the blanket with clenched fingers. She avoided Nadya's eyes as she continued. "He hates witches, but he knows how to rid me of my powers. By marrying him. He says that's what happens when a witch marries a human. It would mean no one need fear me for what I am. It's a service to his people. And me."

The words hung in the air, crackling and threatening thunder. Nadya finally broke the silence. "Why didn't you tell me?"

"I've never wanted to be a witch," cried Katerina. "I won't be a witch, I just . . . I can't!"

"There are worse things to be than a witch," said Nadya. "We can trust Baba Yaga. I'm sure of it."

"You don't understand," said Katerina. "No one has wanted me. This is my chance at a family."

"*We're* family!" said Nadya. She'd never admitted it out loud before, never allowed herself to think it in all the times she'd fantasized about running away into the forest. But it was true. Katerina was her family, the orphanage her home. "And the tsar is threatening *our* home!"

Nadya had a choice. She could stay here as nurse to Katerina, stand by and watch as the tsar hunted Baba Yaga and threatened the village. Or she could warn Baba Yaga and Mrs. Orlova of what was coming.

"Come with me," she said.

Fear flashed in Katerina's eyes. "I can't . . ."

"I'll help you, and Mrs. Orlova. You'll be well again, and—"

"You can't cure me, Nadya. Baba Yaga has cursed me."

"She hasn't," Nadya pleaded. "I'm sure she hasn't!"

"She told me to embrace my magic, the forest. That my life depended on it. What is that but a threat?"

Nadya suddenly felt cold, though the windows were closed and there was a fire in the grate. "What if it was a warning?"

Katerina almost smiled. Her gray face brightened a little. "If it is, then I'll be cured once I marry him. I won't be a witch anymore, and I won't be threatened by powers I no longer have."

"I'll go to her and ask," said Nadya. Katerina's smile had given her hope. "She won't harm me. I'll find out what she meant, why you're sick. But if I'm right, if she didn't curse you, promise me we can ask him to stop the hunt." She pressed her hands on Katerina's arm.

There was a long silence. The doubt on Katerina's face made Nadya's insides ache. But Katerina swallowed and croaked, "We can try. But he might not . . ."

That was all Nadya needed to hear. She leaned forward and hugged Katerina, then grabbed her cloak and the dagger from Baba Yaga and moved toward the door.

With a final wave goodbye, Nadya re-entered the silent

corridor. She gave a small smile to the guards. "Just going to the kitchens—Katerina would like some tea," she said, then raced down the stairs before they had a chance to reply or comment on her outdoor clothes.

She'd only made it to the first landing when something grabbed her arms. The dagger was yanked from her grip.

"Well, well," said the tsar's voice. "Looks like you know more about Baba Yaga than you're letting on. It seems I've underestimated you."

CHAPTER 36

"I really shouldn't be taking you here," said Oksana, her fingers clutching her skirts. "We'll be in so much trouble if anyone sees us."

She led Zima down narrow corridors, up stairs and then down again, her golden hair glimmering in the torchlight. It wasn't the shortest way to the great hall, Oksana said, but it was the way least likely to attract attention. As they turned a final corner, an enormous room opened out before them, its ceiling tall as the sky. Zima stepped onto the wooden floor, and her footsteps echoed as though bouncing off the walls of a canyon.

A door slammed on the far side of the room, and Zima jumped back in surprise. Oksana caught her arm, and together they ducked into the shadows, peering around the corner into the brightness of the great hall.

A group of men marched in, their shoulders square, hands firmly on the swords at their hips. All of them were in uniforms that matched Izel's, except one. A man stood in front with thunder in his expression and lightning in his eyes.

There was a sudden trill in Zima's ears. The voices of the forest had surged, as though something had excited or frightened them. But she couldn't understand what they were telling her.

The man at the front strode into the middle of the room. A cloak the color of midnight whirled behind him as he turned to face the men in uniform who followed behind.

"Rumors have reached me that you were seen with an old woman matching Baba Yaga's description," said the man, sharp as the sword at his side. "Why was she not brought to me?"

Zima followed the man's gaze to see Izel standing in the middle of the group, his arms pinned behind his back by two other large men. He bowed his head, his eyeglasses slipping to the end of his nose. "She was no witch, your illustrious highness." He squeaked in fear, or perhaps it was the effort of lying.

From the way the others looked at the man in the dark cloak and the way Izel bowed his head, this man could only be the tsar.

Everything about him was thick and angular. He had an arrowlike nose poking out over the thick beard. When he stood, it was with one foot in front of the other, as though he were ready to begin moving again. His voice rumbled in his square chest.

"Ah, indeed? See, I know you are lying, because you would not have hidden her from me if you were not," said the tsar. "Tell me, did she curse you?"

Izel shook his head. "No, your illustrious highness."

"Did she overpower you in any other way?" He had lowered his voice, but the words still carried across the room, clear as the shriek of a falcon.

Izel shook his head, his lips pressed closed. His eyes kept darting to the tsar as though he were trying to bravely meet the tsar's gaze, but his quivering jaw gave away his fear.

The tsar nodded his chin at the men holding Izel, then gestured toward the door behind them. One of them gave Izel a sharp punch to the stomach, and as Izel doubled over in pain, they began to drag him away.

Zima wanted to scream. Oksana clapped a hand over her mouth, pulling her back.

The tsar stood, his face now hard as stone. "Take her as well," he said to the guards. Two guards stepped forward. In their arms was a writhing and kicking Nadya.

"You can't do this!" Nadya shouted. "You can't hurt Baba Yaga!"

The tsar's shrill laugh pierced the air.

"What concern is it of yours, little one?" he said, with a look a hawk might give to the mouse in its talons.

"If you hurt Baba Yaga, what are you going to do to Katerina?" she said, venom in her voice.

The tsar didn't answer. He merely smiled at her, as though she'd guessed a delicious secret.

Nadya kicked, and the tsar flinched. "I would advise you to keep quiet in the dungeons. Crying makes the rats hungry."

With that, he swept from the room, his midnight cloak dissolving into the murky darkness of the corridor.

With trembling steps, Zima and Oksana retreated from the horrible scene into a secluded corridor.

Until now, the danger had been only a possibility, something that could be stopped. Like a vision or a frightening dream. But now she could fully imagine the tsar setting fire to the forest, hunting her pack, hunting *her*.

He knew she was here. And she was in danger every second she remained in the castle.

Oksana gripped Zima's shoulders, pulling her out of her thoughts. "We need to get back to the kitchens," she said, and began to steer Zima in that direction.

"No!" Zima reached out to halt Oksana. She was out of time. She couldn't depend on Izel's or Nadya's help anymore. She swallowed, trying to ignore the realization that it was her fault Izel and Nadya were imprisoned. And now it seemed Katerina was in as much danger as the others. "I need you to show me the rest of the way to Katerina's rooms," Zima said.

"You saw what I saw," Oksana mouthed, keeping her voice low. "He is looking for you. It's too dangerous!"

"You're right—he's dangerous," she said. "But something is wrong—I'm worried Katerina is in danger from him."

Oksana bit her lip. "We don't even know her," she said.

"We know him," said Zima. The tsar had shown that he was willing to dispose of anyone who crossed his path. "We can't leave her with him."

Oksana was trembling. She looked as though she could still hear Nadya's screams. But after a moment, she pressed her lips tight and nodded.

Together they trekked in silence down long halls and up winding staircases, past painted walls and carved door-frames. But even the beauty and wonders of the castle couldn't distract Zima from the uneasiness that gnawed at her bones. Compared to the clamor of the kitchen and servants' quarters, these areas were eerily quiet. The only sound was Zima's panting breaths as her old body wrestled with the long walk and steep steps.

Oksana peeked around a corner at a thick wooden door. "The guards are gone," she said in a hushed voice. She unlatched the heavy door and gestured for Zima to follow her, *quickly.*

Zima pressed down the memory of the men dragging
Izel and Nadya to the dungeons.

They entered a room with arched ceilings and painted
walls. The air was thick with the comforting smell of pine
trees. The bed was empty, the vacant room swathed in
shadow.

Snowflakes had begun to sail through the open window
on an icy wind. In front of the window, tied around a bed-
post, was a thick rope matching the fabric of the bedclothes.

Zima dashed to the window. The rope floated down
the wall to the ground below. There was no sign of Katerina anywhere.

CHAPTER 37

Something growled at Baba Yaga from the shadows. A pair of bright eyes narrowed at her.

Snow had begun to fall, and it coated the ground in powdery drifts. Baba Yaga stepped back, and a misplaced paw slipped on one of the patches of ice dotting the ground. She retreated another step. What was this creature? The eyes moved closer, and the shape of a boar emerged from the darkness.

The boar stared at her with angry eyes. She and Ivan must have stumbled into its territory, and it was ready to brutally defend itself. It stamped its hoof, ready to charge. Baba Yaga could almost hear the boar's heartbeat, as rapid and tense as her own—she had never had to defend herself in an attack before. Would she even know how?

She hoped that her wolf instincts would flare up and tell her what to do, but nothing happened. Instead, she tried to make herself as fearsome as she could. Her fur bristled as she brandished her claws and bared her fangs. But the boar was not afraid. It charged.

Baba Yaga leapt over him, and with surprising speed the boar turned, ready to circle her and attack again with the points of its gruesome tusks.

Stop! she called to the creature. *I am the protector of this forest, and you would do well to obey me.*

The boar paused, taking in her words, but dismissed them. Again it stormed toward her, and Baba Yaga backed

into a tree. She ducked to the side to get out of the way, but the boar was too quick. Even in her wolf body she struggled to match its speed. It raged at her, coming closer. She would have to attack.

She raised her paw, uncertain.

The boar squealed as something slammed into its side, sending it tumbling to the ground.

Baba Yaga blinked. Her eyes adjusted. Ivan stood before her, a dagger in one hand and a large stick in the other. He swung the stick at the boar. The creature snorted and charged toward its new enemy. The boy swung the stick again, knocking the boar's hooves out from under it. It hit a tree and shook to right itself, looking dizzied by the unexpected attack.

Ivan withdrew a rope from his pack and deftly tied a loop. As the boar charged at him, he lassoed its front legs. It strained against the rope, but Ivan made a swift knot that held in place. The boar glared with rage in its eyes, but Ivan watched it calmly.

"I have no wish to kill you," he said. "But I won't let you hurt her, or me."

Baba Yaga watched him in surprise. Boar had been known to kill men in sudden attacks, and yet Ivan had stepped in to protect her. Any other human would have run or climbed the nearest tree to escape, but Ivan had stood his ground.

He looked at her. "You have not had to fight a boar before?" he said.

Baba Yaga shook her head. *I am like you—I prefer to leave the forest be.*

"We should put as much distance between us and him as possible," said Ivan, and this time he walked with a steady stride, not wandering as he had done thus far on their journey.

Baba Yaga took a last look at the boar. It watched them in anger. It would escape its ropes sooner or later, but if they were far enough away, it would not track them.

She sprinted to catch up with Ivan. The icy ground was hard against her paws.

They walked for some minutes in silence. Baba Yaga paused, allowing him to lead, and she couldn't help but notice that Ivan stood taller, more sure-footed. He sidestepped thorns and leapt with agility over unexpected pits half-concealed by bushes and branches. He no longer seemed in danger of being taken by surprise by the forest. Even the snowdrifts and ice slicks didn't faze him.

She had thought him too weak to defeat the tsar, but he had not hesitated to put himself in harm's way to protect her. He had demonstrated in these few days together that he was more of a leader than she had ever been in her hundreds of years as Baba Yaga.

Ivan deserved to know the truth from her.

They could not be far from the hut now, a few hours at

most. The sky was painted with swirling gray clouds that would obscure the rising full moon. She had already waited too long to tell him.

As she trotted to catch up with him, Ivan stopped and took a seat on a fallen tree, grabbing some thick brown bread from his sack. His movements were sharp and agitated.

Baba Yaga crept close to him, watching his face as he ate silently. There was anger in his eyes, which surprised her.

We need to keep moving, she said. They had to get to the hut tonight.

Ivan's head jerked to look away from her imploring eyes. "I am done walking for the night."

We are so close, pleaded Baba Yaga.

Ivan's eyes snapped to her. "Why are we rushing? This was my request. And I don't even know if I want it anymore."

No, no, they couldn't give up now. Not when they were nearly there.

What's wrong? she said.

He ignored her at first, but when she asked again, he said at last, "When that boar attacked, you said it should obey you. Why is that?"

Baba Yaga averted her gaze.

"You are more than an ordinary wolf," he said. "It's not just that you can speak." He took a bite of his bread and glared at her. "Have you lied to me? Were you ever taking me to Baba Yaga?"

Baba Yaga looked at her paws. *No,* she said. *And yes.*

His shoulders tensed, and a muscle began to twitch near his temple. He stood and started to pace around the clearing. "What do you mean?"

I am taking you to Baba Yaga's hut, as I promised, she said. *But there is something I haven't told you.* She took a deep breath. *I am Baba Yaga.*

His brow furrowed as he took in her words. "You're what?"

I have been searching for you, because I know who you are—I have always known.

"You are Baba Yaga, and you didn't tell me?" He kicked at the fallen bough, dislodging fresh snow. "My grandmother was right," he said, and he turned to look at her, not anger but disappointment contorting his features. "You're a liar."

She was right, said Baba Yaga. *Your family lost everything because of me. But has she told you* what *you lost?*

"Our home," said Ivan.

It is more than that, said Baba Yaga. *Your great-grandfather was the tsar. Your family was forced to flee the castle because he was murdered. The murderer had help from me.*

"I'm . . . he was . . . the tsar? What my grandmother said about our home, it was the castle?" The shock in his eyes shifted to anger. Ivan's hands balled into fists, his legs shaking. "How could you? Why would you do that?"

I was tricked, said Baba Yaga. *I had no wish to see him*

dethroned. But a man used my own magic against me, and co-erced me into telling him how to steal the tsardom.

"But why didn't you prevent it?" said Ivan.

Baba Yaga looked away from him. She couldn't bring herself to admit the true reason: that she hadn't cared enough to stop him.

For so long she'd been content to stay in her hut and let the problems of the outside world pass her by as though they didn't concern her. But they did. The forest was now in danger because of her mistake—no, her choice. Of all the evils in the world, the greatest was the temptation of the easy path over the right one.

Ivan took a step back from her. His kind face was twisted by a look of disgust. "What were you planning when we reached your hut?" he said.

There is a dagger there, one that will always seek the blood of a tsar, she said. *I intended to give you that dagger, and tell you your true origin. The current tsar now threatens this forest. My hope was that you would stop him.*

"Instead of stopping him yourself" was Ivan's retort. "He threatens this forest because you allowed his family to steal the throne that belonged to my family. And still you're not facing him—you wish me to do it for you."

Baba Yaga winced at the truth in his words.

"And what if I don't want the tsardom? What if I want a quiet life—what if I'd rather stay at home?"

Baba Yaga answered softly, *If he is successful in his plans, the entire forest is in danger. He must be stopped.*

"Then you stop him," he spat. "I can't continue on this journey with you. Not after you've lied to me. How do I even know you're telling the truth now?"

You don't, she said. *But what I say is true. If you won't do it for me, then do it for the forest you love.*

She closed her eyes, trying to quiet the heartbreak fermenting inside her. The sounds of heavy footsteps and the thrashing of branches made her flinch.

When she opened her eyes again, Ivan was gone.

She was all alone, no better off than she had been when she started.

And the threat of the tsar loomed ever closer.

CHAPTER 38

Katerina was gone.

Zima leaned out the window searching for footprints in the newly fallen snow, but there was no sign of her. The icy breeze made her eyes water as it blasted her wispy hair away from her face.

Rolling hills stretched out before the castle, and the road snaked over the landscape toward the village. Below the window, servants were carting firewood and supplies for the wedding across the castle grounds, but Zima saw no trace of Katerina among them. They would notice her disappearance soon.

Off to the left, the forest stretched to where the earth met the sky, the tips of the trees rippling like the waters of an enormous lake. Had Katerina entered the forest, or had she followed the road to the village? Could she even navigate the snow in her condition?

Zima latched the window shut and turned to the door, but before she'd taken another step, a flapping sound made her stop.

It was the raven, perched on the back of a carved wooden chair. *Here you are,* he snapped, waving his wings in agitation. *Have you any idea the danger you're in? You were supposed to stay in the hut.*

"Quiet, someone might hear you!" Zima hissed. She looked back at Oksana, who was staring in wonder and curiosity at what must have been a very strange scene. Zima put her hands on her hips and said to the raven in a low voice, "I heard the tsar was planning a hunt, and I didn't want to stay in the hut and wait for the forest to catch fire around me."

We need to get you to the hut, right away, the raven said. *Baba Yaga will have returned by now, and the spell must be done tonight.*

Zima crept closer to him, struggling to understand what he'd just said. "Baba Yaga is back? What do you mean—what spell must be done?"

The raven fluttered toward the window and nodded up at a sliver of moonlight piercing the heavy clouds. *The moon seals magic.*

That's right, Zima remembered this from the memory in

the cauldron, when Baba Yaga swore to Tsar Aleksander's great-grandfather that she would always tell him the truth. What might have been an ordinary promise was made magical by moonlight.

He gave Zima a very pointed look. *That means a spell becomes irreversible at the full moon.*

She still didn't understand.

The raven moved his feet in an irritated sort of dance and sighed. *That means if you and she are not in your old bodies by sunrise, the spell is permanent.*

Zima might as well have plunged through ice into a freezing lake. Every part of her was in shock. "Why—why didn't you tell me?"

Because she knew she'd be back by now, and—the raven clicked his beak—*you were not supposed to leave the hut!*

Zima glanced out the window. The sun had set, but it was only early evening, and the cold season's nights were long-lasting. She still had time.

"We will go to the hut, but there's something I have to do first!" She pressed an ear to the door and, when all was silent, stepped into the hall, pausing to let the raven land on her shoulder.

What could possibly be so impor—

"Hush!" There wasn't time to explain to him about Nadya and Izel and why Zima had to save them. To her surprise, the raven closed his beak (though he gave her a very dirty look). She turned to Oksana, who seemed surprisingly calm about just having witnessed a conversation between a witch and her raven. "Can you lead me to the dungeons?"

Oksana was disconcerted by *that* anyway. "But if the tsar—"

"You can leave here with us," said Zima. "You would be safer in my hut."

The young baker bit her lip as she often did, but then she nodded and led them from the room.

Together the group crept through the darkened corridors. They entered the great hall, then ducked through the door where Izel had been dragged away. A howling draft whipped up the steps.

Zima clutched at the stone walls with one hand and gripped her cane in the other as they descended curving stairs. The air was thick with damp.

At last, they approached a door that looked as heavy as the tree that had made it. When Zima turned the handle, the door swung away and slammed against a wall. She crept forward and they were swallowed by darkness.

CHAPTER 39

Nadya was trapped and alone. She wanted to claw at the stone walls holding her in like an animal, but she couldn't bring herself to move. Tiny rat claws skittered on the stone floors nearby, and from above, the eyes of hanging bats blinked in the dim light.

She had failed. Not only in her promise to Baba Yaga to stop the hunt, but now Katerina was in danger too. And Nadya was trapped here, unable to do anything about it.

Izel was the only other prisoner, also accused of helping Baba Yaga. They'd each tried to pick their cell's locks at first, but as darkness fell and shadows surrounded them, they both grew quiet and still.

The clank of a latch and the groan of a door opening at the entrance to the dungeon made her jump. "Who's there?" she said. Her voice quivered like a leaf in a breeze.

"Nadya?" someone whispered. The voice was familiar. Creaky as an old tree.

Izel spoke from the cell beside Nadya's. "Baba Yaga?" he said.

Relief washed over Nadya. Baba Yaga was safe, and she was here in the dungeon. Not as a prisoner, Nadya hoped.

"Where can I find the keys?" said a female voice Nadya didn't recognize.

"Through the far door," said Izel.

The whispers made Nadya's skin prickle, bringing warmth and comfort to the damp chill of her cell. How had Baba Yaga even managed to find her?

It made her feel even worse that she'd failed Baba Yaga, promising to help and losing sight of that promise. Baba Yaga was still here, even though Nadya hadn't done what she'd said she would do, and now there was no way to stop the tsar's hunt.

Nadya wished she didn't make so many mistakes, especially the ones that hurt other people. Not because she believed this would make them love her, but because she loved them. She could try harder. She could do better.

"Baba Yaga?" Nadya asked.

"Yes?"

"I'm so sorry for—" Before she could finish, Nadya was bathed in orange light. She blinked and shielded her eyes.

The door on the far wall had opened, and three of the tsar's soldiers stood in the doorway. Torches lining the hall behind them threw an eerie glow into the dungeon and cast shadows over their faces.

"Step away," said the guard at the front.

Even Baba Yaga's wrinkles seemed to scowl as she looked at the guards. She held out a protective arm, shielding the young woman beside her wearing a servant's uniform. For the first time, Nadya understood why people were so afraid of the witch.

"Keep back," said Baba Yaga to the guards. "I will curse you if you take another step. . . ."

The guard at the front laughed. He was big as a boulder and covered in mosslike hair. "You think I fear your tree magic?" He turned to the others and pretended to shiver and tremble. "Oh no, I might get scratched by thorns or tripped by roots!"

The others grunted with laughter.

"The tsar told us about your *magic*," said the guard, stepping forward. "So go ahead, curse me."

Nadya screamed and threw her weight against the bars as one of the guards lunged for Baba Yaga. The bars held fast. Nadya was trapped, forced to watch as the guards attacked the old witch.

Baba Yaga backed up against the wall. Her raven leapt from her shoulder and swooped toward one guard, beating his wings and pecking at the guard with his sharp beak.

Before Nadya could fully understand what was happening, Baba Yaga swung her cane over her head. The instant it connected with the guard, the air rippled through the room with a jolt that made the metal bars of her cell ring.

Baba Yaga dropped her cane and collapsed forward, cradling her hands. The servant girl rushed to her side.

Nadya covered her eyes. She couldn't bear it if the guards had hurt Baba Yaga.

But there was only stillness. Nadya looked up.

Three large boulders stood where the guards had been. They no longer resembled humans at all.

The raven swooped back to Baba Yaga and dropped something in front of her. It clinked and clattered against the stone floor. The key ring.

Baba Yaga picked it up, shuffled forward, and began shoving keys into the lock of Nadya's cell. Finally the door swung open with a squeal. Without a word Nadya staggered forward and threw her arms around the witch. Baba Yaga stiffened at first, then softened and placed her palms on Nadya's shoulders. When they broke their hug, Nadya saw that the servant girl was smiling.

Nadya wanted to ask the question that had been plaguing her since her conversation with Katerina. Baba Yaga had now helped Nadya twice. Could the witch really be the cause of Katerina's illness? But before she could ask, Baba

Yaga's expression darkened, the shadows deepening her many wrinkles. "Katerina is missing. We went to her first, but she seems to have run away."

Fear and hope swelled up in Nadya's heart. Maybe Katerina had decided to leave the tsar after all. But what would the tsar think? Would his hunt now include Katerina too?

"The tsar is searching for you," she said to Baba Yaga. "It's why he put us in here."

Izel nodded. "We must get you somewhere safe." He grabbed a torch and gestured for the others to follow him, through a passage on the far wall and down a long corridor. The raven landed on Izel's shoulder, as if eager to lead the way.

Along dim halls they went, up steps and then down, unlocking gates and doors with the keys from the stolen ring. Nadya was dizzy with all the twists and turns. They walked for so long that it seemed impossible they were still within the castle walls. She looked for a window to check where they were, but there were none. She realized there hadn't been any windows along the whole corridor. In fact, it was no longer a corridor at all.

Somehow, without realizing it, they'd entered a tunnel to a cave. Rough stone jutted down, and their footsteps over the uneven ground echoed in her ears.

"Where are you taking us?" Nadya asked him.

He didn't respond, only pointing ahead, where the

passage began to slope upward. Wind wailed past them as they rounded a final turn and then emerged into open air.

For a moment there was perfect silence. Then the cry of a fox, the heavy hoofbeats of nearby elk. Leaves whirled and crackled past them, and Nadya's nose was filled with the familiar smells of pine needles and mushrooms mixed with the bite of frost.

All around them was the glow of snow in the light of Izel's torch. It clumped in little piles where it fell between gaps in the tree branches.

"We're in the forest," said Nadya in awe. The raven let out a screech of delight and swooped up to land on a tree branch.

"There are several passages that lead out of the castle," said Izel. He looked around and took a deep breath, filling his lungs with the sweet night air. "Many years ago, before Tsar Aleksander's family came into power, the old tsar and tsaritsa loved the forest. It is said they would use these passages often to travel to their favorite meadows and glens. I think I'm the only one who uses them now."

Izel then retreated into the darkness of the cave, his face thrust into shadow. "I am glad to see you safe," he said to Baba Yaga. "I hope that those who remain in the castle will soon be freed from the tsar, thanks to you."

An unreadable expression flashed across Baba Yaga's face. She gave a slow and hesitant nod.

Nadya reached toward him. "You should come with us. What if the tsar finds you?" Her stomach twisted at the thought of returning to the dangers of the castle when they'd just escaped its dungeons.

But Izel shook his head. "I must make sure others—my wife—are safe first."

The servant girl stepped toward him. "I can help you," she said.

Baba Yaga protested, placing a hand on the girl's arm and holding tight. "It's too dangerous, Oksana. What if he realizes you helped me?"

Nadya couldn't help but agree, even if she didn't know how this girl had helped Baba Yaga. Both Izel and Oksana would be safer in the woods with Baba Yaga and Nadya.

But Oksana stood firm. She brushed a strand of golden hair away from her face and placed her hand on top of Baba Yaga's. "We have to warn the other servants. They're all in danger from the tsar's wrath."

Izel nodded. "Do not worry, we will join you," he said to Baba Yaga. He gave Nadya what might have been a wink of reassurance. "We won't let you face him alone. I know all will be well," he said, smiling warmly, "with you on our side."

With that, Izel and Oksana left Nadya alone with Baba Yaga, disappearing into the passage back to the castle.

CHAPTER 40

Zima watched Izel and Oksana go, the man's words ring-ing in her mind. They were depending on her. They had seen her do magic. She could still feel the hum and tingle in her hands from fending off the guards in the dungeons.

It had frightened her, when she'd first arrived at the cas-tle, how Izel was looking to her to protect them from the tsar. Somehow she'd gotten this far. Her heart gave a twinge. Perhaps this was how Grom felt, with everyone in the pack looking up to him. Whenever Zima saw him again, she would ask him. That is, if she could find a way to see him again.

She stepped forward out of the mouth of the cave, and her warm thoughts were driven away as the full force of the winter storm seized her. What looked like gently wafting snowflakes now stung her cheeks and hands. An icy wind howled past, whipping her cloak and skirts. They needed to get out of this storm.

Call the hut! shouted the raven. His words were swept away by the moaning wind.

Of course. The hut would keep them warm and take them wherever they needed to go. The raven had said that the hut would come when Baba Yaga called it, that it would help when needed. And she needed help.

But could it navigate this storm?

Zima tucked her cane under her arm and rubbed her hands together. The knuckles had grown stiff and sore in the cold. Then she held them in the air and called, "House!" She paused, thinking of a compliment, some way to flatter the house into coming to her aid. "I need your swift legs and strong walls!" Her words were carried away as quickly as she uttered them.

She stood frozen, her hands still raised, hoping that the house was close enough to hear her call. Her stomach squeezed harder with each passing second. What if the hut didn't come? Where would they go?

One minute passed. Then two.

She lowered her hands and held them close to her chest to warm them. The hut wasn't coming.

And then she heard it.

A distant thumping sound bashed through the trees.

Zima's heart jumped to its rhythm. *Thump thump thump thump.*
Tree branches snapped and creaked. The ground rumbled.

It appeared in the distance, the firelight shining through
its windows, paying no attention to the branches or boughs
that stood in its way. It collided with and bounced off immovable trunks, stumbled, and carried on. The bright-
orange chicken legs took long, loping steps, sometimes
lifting themselves so high they nearly smacked the bottom
of the house.

As the house drew near, the chicken feet dug in their
heels and skidded over the icy earth. The legs lowered the
hut and the steps pivoted out and down, revealing the front

door. It was hard to tell, but the steps, which always made Zima think of a mouth, seemed to be smiling.

She and Nadya climbed into the hut's warmth. Everything was exactly as she had left it. All the skulls and trinkets sat in their usual places on the shelves, and the bucket of rocks was tucked into its corner. A fire crackled in the hearth.

She's not here, said the raven.

He was right. The hut was empty.

"You said she'd be here," said Zima.

I know I did, he snapped. He fluttered over to the mantel and scratched his claws on the wood. *Where is she?*

"How should I know? You only just told me she planned to come back tonight."

But the raven was giving her an odd look. *How did you figure it out?*

Zima blinked at him. "Figure out what?"

He fluttered forward. *Baba Yaga's object. You can do magic now.*

Zima stared at him. She'd done magic, first when healing Oksana, and then again in the dungeons. She remembered the tingling in her hands as she'd gripped—

"The cane." She looked down at the carved wooden staff. It had helped her move in this witch's body, and apparently in other ways as well. "I—I didn't mean to," she stammered. "I know it was the last of Baba Yaga's rules—"

That doesn't matter anymore. The full moon is tonight.

Katerina is missing. And Baba Yaga hasn't returned. Don't you understand what this means?

"What are you saying?"

You have to be Baba Yaga now.

Zima nearly fell backward. "No—I can't possibly—"

A little voice beside her made her jump. "What's wrong, Baba Yaga?"

Nadya. Zima had almost forgotten she was in the room.

"I . . ." Zima wondered how to explain what the raven had told her. "I might be trapped as Baba Yaga."

"But you've always been Baba Yaga," said Nadya. She wasn't saying this in confusion, but with the certainty of truth.

"I didn't used to be. I used to be"—she paused, wondering how Nadya would react—"a wolf. Called Zima. I hope to be a wolf again someday."

Nadya looked thoughtful. "Is that the family you meant? Your pack?"

Zima nodded.

"Like the wolf who visits me in the village?" asked Nadya.

Veter. Zima smiled. "Yes. He's my friend."

There was a loud tapping sound from the mantel. The raven was knocking his beak against the wood to get her attention. *We need to find Katerina. She is somewhere out there*—he gestured with a wing toward the window and the howling storm outside—*and the tsar will be looking for her. As you're the new Baba Yaga, I follow your orders.*

"I am not the new Baba Yaga!" Zima shouted, stamping a foot. "I am a wolf, and I will be a wolf again."

Why did you trade places with Baba Yaga? asked the raven.

"To save my brother."

Now you need to save the forest. This is about more than you and me. It's about all of us.

Zima opened her mouth to argue, but he shushed her, and pointed with his beak at the cauldron. *You don't understand. Ask it. Ask it to show you his true plans.*

"I know his plans," said Zima. "He wants to hunt Baba Yaga."

That's not everything, said the raven. *Ask the cauldron. You'll see.*

The memory of her first day in the hut sprang into her mind, when the cauldron had showed her Baba Yaga's memory. Zima pulled herself upright and crept toward the fireplace, Nadya following close beside her. Steam beaded on the end of her chin as she leaned over the bubbling liquid. Hints of pine needles and honey entered her nose.

She took the spoon from its hook, dipped it just below the surface, and stirred.

"What are the tsar's true plans?" she grunted to the cauldron. She felt Nadya's hands close around her arm.

The grayish-brown lumps bobbed about, swimming in circles, and then all at once they were gone.

The whole hut disappeared around her, like a lightning

flash that brought darkness instead of light. After an instant the hut reappeared, but everything was different. Sunlight streamed through the windows. Standing at opposite ends of the table, staring at each other, were Baba Yaga and Tsar Aleksander. Neither of them glanced at Zima or Nadya.

"I did not invite you in," said Baba Yaga to Tsar Aleksander, her lip curling into a sneer.

The tsar returned the gaze without any hint of concern. "But you must answer my question," the tsar said, "whether you wish to or not."

Baba Yaga's eyes narrowed. "I thought this curse was long forgotten by your family."

A look of disgust crossed the tsar's face. "My parents and grandparents were good to me, they protected me. But they couldn't see how the bargain my great-grandfather made with you wasn't a gift—it was a prison."

Tsar Aleksander leaned forward, intensity burning in his eyes. "My castle, my tsardom, everything that is mine comes from your"—he twirled his fingers—"your earth magic. So many years of my childhood were spent hiding away in a castle, fearing the threat of this evil forest, watching it creep closer to our home. Coming to take back what it had given."

He watched Baba Yaga as though he expected her to contradict him, but she stayed silent. He continued, "I tried setting fire to it, but its magic was too strong. It always healed itself before I could get very far. And then I realized"—he held his hand to his forehead in mock amazement—"*I could ask you*. 'A truthful answer, always,' not just for my great-grandfather, but for his whole family."

Baba Yaga pressed her hands flat against the tabletop. Her purple-flecked eyes flashed. "And what is your question?" she asked.

The tsar pulled out a chair and sat down, laying his fur cloak over the arm. He leaned back casually, fingers tracing the top of his beard as he considered his response.

Finally, a wicked grin twisted his angular features. He leaned forward and spoke in a voice so low that Zima had to step toward him to hear. "How can I destroy the forest?" he said.

Baba Yaga's expression was unchanged, but her hands pressed against the table until the knuckles turned white. She took a long time to answer.

At last, she exhaled. Her breath came out in shuddering gasps.

The tsar laughed. It was flat and without humor. "You cannot avoid the question, so why resist it? It will only tire you, old woman."

Baba Yaga was clearly fighting not to say the words that followed, but they escaped in a raspy voice. "I am the forest's protector. To destroy it you would have to kill me."

Tsar Aleksander smiled, then he stood and pulled a

dagger from its sheath. The jeweled hilt gleamed. He traced the blade under Baba Yaga's chin. "So I could kill you now."

Baba Yaga didn't answer. Her face was calm, unmoving, a stone against a storm.

For a moment, doubt flickered across the tsar's face. But it only lasted an instant. He straightened his arm, and the dagger point dug into Baba Yaga's flesh. "There must be more. Tell me how to kill you."

"The forest decides when it is my time. Only magic can kill me. To obtain it, you must find my successor, and perform the binding ceremony just before dawn at the full moon. This will allow you to share in her magic."

The tsar raised a pointed brow. "Ceremony?"

"A ceremony to bind human and witch together until the witch's life ends. There are several, but the most well-known is a wedding."

Beside Zima, Nadya gasped. The tsar's eyes lingered on Baba Yaga's wrinkled hands. "And where can I find this new Baba Yaga?"

Again, Baba Yaga fought to answer him. She gripped the table until tendrils and vines began to sprout from it. Her eyes bulged and her lips darkened as she pressed them tight to contain the secrets within her.

There was a screech and a flash of black feathers. The raven swooped through the air toward the tsar's hand and snatched the dagger in his claws. He darted into the rafters of the little hut, hidden from view.

And that's when Zima recognized it. The dagger, the one she'd given Nadya as a gift for the tsar. Without realizing it, she'd returned it to him.

The tsar didn't move to snatch it back. Instead, he kept his eyes locked on Baba Yaga, waiting for her answer.

The witch exhaled, gasping, her face pale.

"In the village. A young woman named Katerina." She trembled as she uttered the words.

"Excellent. You've been most instructive," said the tsar, rising and kicking the chair out of his way as he moved toward the door.

A clatter made Zima jump. Baba Yaga had leapt to her feet and her cane had fallen to the floor. "You cannot take her!" the witch cried. "She doesn't understand what she is. She was raised as a human."

The tsar rewrapped his fur cloak about his shoulders. It was wolf fur, black and sleek. "Then she knows what all humans know . . . never trust a witch."

Baba Yaga's expression suddenly changed, her eyes glazed. She was watching the cloak, seeing it, but not seeing it. *"Find the gray wolf . . . ,"* she muttered.

"What did you say?" snapped the tsar.

"Nothing . . . ," she said, though power flowed in her words. Baba Yaga glanced upward at the raven. "That dagger belonged to the old tsar," she said. "Everything you're protecting is stolen. Everything you have is an illusion. You are at the mercy of the forest. It is coming for you."

"Not for long, my dear old witch," said Tsar Aleksander. "Soon the forest will be at my mercy." He smirked, and with a final flick of his wolf cloak left the hut.

As the door drifted closed, Baba Yaga threw it open wide and shouted, "The forest has a plan. You will be defeated by a gray wolf!"

But it was too late. The tsar was gone.

Zima blinked. Smoke filled her eyes. The fire was roaring, and the liquid in the cauldron bubbled furiously. Nadya was still clutching her arm with trembling fingers. "Baba Ya— I mean, Zima, we have to do something!"

The whispers seemed to agree. They swelled inside Zima. She felt a bit sick. "If the tsar marries Katerina," Zima asked the raven, "will he have her magic?"

The raven nodded, and Nadya squeezed Zima's arm so tightly it began to ache. *He can command the forest as well as destroy it. He might discover he enjoys the power more. And all of us will be under his control.*

Her mind was spinning. "Couldn't Baba Yaga have hidden Katerina away? Kept her safe?"

She tried, but Katerina wouldn't listen. Baba Yaga couldn't force her to come to the forest; her magic wouldn't control another witch like that. Katerina has to embrace her magic willingly.

A growl of frustration rumbled in Zima's throat. "Why is your friend so stubborn?" she snapped at Nadya.

Nadya looked startled, and she became even more unsettled when Zima explained what the raven had said. "Can she protect herself?" Nadya asked. "Can her magic shield her from him?"

Zima thought about this for a moment. It seemed unlikely, since Katerina wasn't willing to embrace her magic, like the raven said. But maybe she could do magic without realizing, just as Zima had. "She would need an object, something of the forest, like my cane. Does she have anything like that?"

She waited as Nadya began to pace the small room. At last, she stopped, her shoulders slumped. "No, I can't think of anything."

Zima turned back to the raven. "I don't understand, why didn't Baba Yaga stop him? Use her magic on him like I did in the dungeon?"

Don't you get it? said the raven, flapping his wings in exasperation. *The forest wanted you. She couldn't do this alone. She had to find you.*

"Was I just a tool for Baba Yaga to carry out her plans?"

She never wanted to place you in danger.

She eyed Nadya, who was watching them in fear and

confusion, unable to understand his words, but clearly catching their urgency all the same. "I *am* in danger. We all are," said Zima. A fire that had sparked to life while watching the memory was now raging in her mind, wild and hungry. She moved to the window and looked outside. It was the middle of the night now—too much time had passed already. "You're right. I have to stop this."

What would you have me do? said the raven.

"Search the forest," said Zima. They needed to make sure Katerina was safe from the tsar. "We have to find her before he does."

The raven bowed. *You will stop him,* he said. *The forest knew all along.* Then he flapped his wings, gliding toward the window and kicking open the latch with his clawed foot. Once outside he rose high into the air, his dark feathers becoming one with the night.

Zima was grateful for the raven's help, but it did nothing to soothe the uneasiness in her mind. The forest was a big place, and they needed to find Katerina quickly. Would he be able to trace her in time, searching on his own?

"How can we help find her?" Zima asked Nadya.

Nadya pulled out a map she'd been working on that showed the forest as seen from a great height, with the road winding along the edge of the trees between the castle and the village. "She must be going to the village," said Nadya. "And the road is the quickest way."

The road was also the most exposed. Trying to navigate it in this storm would be near impossible.

They tried other ideas. First the cauldron, without success, then Zima asked the house to search for her. It gave a sad shudder, as though it didn't know how. If Nadya was right and Katerina wasn't in the forest, then the forest magic might be struggling to find her. That would also mean the raven was looking in the wrong place.

Not for the first time, Zima longed for her wolf nose. Baba Yaga couldn't track Katerina in a snowstorm, but Zima's wolf body could have. If only Grom didn't hate witches, she could ask him for help.

She paused. Grom might not help, but Veter would.

She looked to Nadya. "We need something that would have her scent. Do you have anything that belongs to her?"

"There must be something at the orphanage." Nadya thought for a moment, then her face brightened. "She gave me a doll before she went away."

A plan had begun to grow. Everything would be okay. Zima looked up to the rafters. It was a shame the house couldn't leave the forest. Its swift legs would have made shorter work of the task of finding Katerina. But all the same, it could help. "House," she said, "take us as close as you can to the orphanage."

CHAPTER 41

now was falling fast now, the winter winds forming
drifts two- and three-feet deep. Ivan wouldn't last the
night in this storm.

Baba Yaga needed to get to her hut. From there, she
could find him. Even if Ivan refused to aid in defeating
the tsar, she could at least prevent him from freezing to
death.

But something was wrong. She was near the place where
she'd left her hut, yet there was no smell of magic. Her hut
had been moved.

A growl escaped her. That wolf had been messing
with magic.

Lifting her nose to the air, Baba Yaga searched for a hint of the right scent.

The winds shifted and she caught it: the resinous smell of magic and moonlight.

CHAPTER 42

Snow blasted into the hut as Zima opened the front door. Together she and Nadya, clutching warm cloaks around their shoulders, descended the steps to the forest floor. Their feet sank into powdery snow. Wading through it was like trudging through water, fighting against a current.

The hut had taken them right to the edge of the forest. Ahead, the trees thinned, and torchlight signaled the border of the village. With careful steps, they crossed the snowy hill toward the orphanage. Something bounded toward Zima and Nadya where they stood, and Zima recognized the wolf's familiar trot.

Veter!

Baba Yaga! he said, his tail wagging. *What are you doing here?*

"Looking for you," said Zima. She felt warm at the sight of him. If she'd still had her tail, it would have wagged too.

Me? he said.

"I need your help," she said. But there was something else she had to say first. She'd spent the last week pretending that she was someone she wasn't. It was time to tell the truth about what she'd done. "Veter, I have something to tell you," said Zima.

His eye glittered in the pale light as he looked up at her, curious.

She paused for such a long time that Veter finally asked, *What is it?*

"I'm Zima."

There was no hint of surprise or astonishment on his face. He simply stared at her, taking her in, as if seeing her for the first time. Then at last he let out a yip of delight.

I knew you reminded me of her! There was laughter in his voice.

"You're not horrified? That I made this trade with the witch? You don't blame me?"

Blame you? he said. *I should have been there with you. You are the closest thing I have to a pack . . .* He paused before saying, *Zima.* Then he added, *It will be strange calling you by your real name, though.*

Zima knelt next to him and put her neck against his, as she might have when she was a wolf. The feel of his fur and the warmth of his breath filled her with comfort and strength. When she stood, he rubbed against Nadya in greeting. Nadya giggled and reached out to stroke his fur.

"How are the rest of my pack, Veter?" Zima asked, almost afraid to hear the answer. "Have you seen them?"

Veter stiffened. He pulled away from Nadya.

"I'm sorry," said Zima. "Did I say—"

Zima, now I must tell you something, why I didn't run away from the village, Veter said, suddenly breathless. *It's your pack. They want to attack the village. That was Grom's plan all along.*

How could she have missed it? The day that Leto was stabbed after going to the village, it wasn't just about taking weapons. Grom had succeeded in his plan to make the humans defenseless against the wolves. But as a consequence, he'd also left them vulnerable to the tsar.

"Then we'll be here to stop them," said Zima, managing to keep her voice calm in spite of the fluttering in her chest. At a confused look from Nadya, she took the girl's hand and squeezed it. She'd explain to Nadya later, but for now, she didn't want her to feel threatened and frightened by the wolves' planned attack. They had to focus on Katerina. "But first there's something else we have to do."

What is it? asked Veter.

She told him that Katerina was lost in the forest and the tsar intended to use her for her powers.

Veter's brow furrowed, and for a moment Zima felt fear rise in her throat that his new trust of witches didn't extend to Katerina. Instead, he said, *What can we do?*

"We need to find her, before he does," she said.

CHAPTER 43

Together Nadya, Zima, and Nadya's wolf, who she'd learned was called Veter, crunched through the snow toward the orphanage. She opened the kitchen door as quietly as possible, taking care to avoid letting the latch clatter or the hinges squeak. Everyone would be asleep, and the last thing Nadya needed was to frighten anyone at the sight of the wolf.

Nadya's heart thumped at the joy of seeing her wolf again. Zima had explained that he had agreed to help them find Katerina.

She left Zima and Veter downstairs in the warmth by the oven while she crept up to the bedroom where she'd left Katerina's doll. But as she approached her old room, soft candlelight spilled out, and she entered to find Mrs. Orlova awake, seated on Nadya's bed.

"Nadya?" the matron whispered. Her eyes flitted to the other girls, who were still snoring.

Nadya stepped forward. The instant the light hit her face, Mrs. Orlova rushed toward her, clutching her shoulders, then pulling her close.

The matron snatched a candle from a nearby table and together they stepped out onto the landing, pulling the door closed behind them.

"You foolish girl!" she whispered. "I thought I'd lost you to the woods."

"You did," said Nadya. It was hard to believe that only a few days ago she had run away.

The flame from Mrs. Orlova's candle lit the tears that trickled down her cheeks. "I am sorry I didn't have more faith in you to impress the tsar," she said. "I suppose, in a way, I didn't want to lose both you and Katerina."

At the mention of the tsar, Nadya's heart skipped a beat. Mrs. Orlova listened to Nadya's hurried explanation that Katerina had run away from the castle.

"We'll find her," she replied, looking more determined than Nadya had ever seen her. "Come, let's harness the sleigh."

Nadya quietly ducked into the room and retrieved Katerina's doll. Hopefully, there were enough traces of Katerina's scent for Veter to be able to track her in the snow.

Together they rushed down the stairs. But as they reached the bottom step, Mrs. Orlova froze, staring at the witch and the wolf in the middle of her kitchen. Snowflakes had melted off them to form puddles at their feet.

"Stay behind me," said Mrs. Orlova, reaching for Nadya's shoulder.

But Nadya shook her head. "They're going to help us." She reached out with the doll toward Veter and laid it on the floor at his paws. Mrs. Orlova stiffened at her side. But the wolf merely gave it a sniff, then looked up to Zima, his nose twitching. He barked.

"Can he smell Katerina?" Nadya asked.

Zima gave a low chuckle. "He says it smells like magic. Like me."

Nadya gave a sideways glance at Mrs. Orlova, who didn't seem all too surprised by the news. The matron's expression remained cold and wary. "Do you think he can track her?" Nadya asked Zima.

Zima opened the door, and freezing air flooded the room. The wolf bounded outside, lifting his nose and zigzagging away, leaving a trail of paw prints in the snow as he ascended a nearby hill. He let out a series of short howls.

Zima turned to Nadya, a faint hope shining in her wrinkled smile. "He can smell her," she said.

"Then I will go with you," said Mrs. Orlova, and she

went to retrieve her cloak. Whatever distrust she had of this witch, finding Katerina was more important.

Together Mrs. Orlova and Nadya readied the sleigh, piling it full of warm blankets and hitching on their single horse from the barn. He was old, but strong, and must have sensed their nervousness, because he stamped on the ground while they worked, warming his muscles and blowing puffs of foggy air from his nostrils.

As Nadya opened the barn door, she eyed the rolling hills that separated the village from the castle, with the forest forming a jagged border on the right. If Katerina had taken the road, there would be no trees to protect her from the winter weather or the tsar's search parties.

Mrs. Orlova flicked the reins and the horse trotted forward, the sleigh gliding over the snow behind him. They slowed, and Mrs. Orlova moved to help Zima up into the sleigh.

"I'm coming too!" said Nadya, scrambling to sit beside the witch.

"Go inside, Nadya," said Mrs. Orlova. "This is too dangerous."

Heat filled Nadya's cheeks. "I won't let Katerina get hurt," she said defiantly. She was tired of trying to please Mrs. Orlova, Katerina, everyone. This was what she needed to do. The truth of it chimed in her bones. It didn't matter if she was in the orphanage, or in the forest, or in the castle. What mattered was that she, and Katerina, and Mrs. Orlova were safe from the tsar.

A battle raged on Mrs. Orlova's face, but she finally relented. "Stay close to me."

Nadya opened her mouth to argue, but then she realized that Mrs. Orlova had given in. She smiled. It felt good, standing up for herself.

CHAPTER 44

"Can you still smell her?" Zima called to Veter.

In answer, Veter made a snuffling sound and set forth, bounding up a slope with his nose leading the way. Mrs. Orlova guided the horse to follow, weaving between the hills. The sleigh sliced through the snow as Veter bounded around the high drifts. Cold scratched at Zima's cheeks. She pulled the cloak more tightly around her shoulders.

After the sleigh had glided over and around several hills, Zima's lips had gone numb, and she had to shout to be heard above the wind. "Is she close?"

I think so! said Veter.

He picked up speed, gaining momentum as the scent grew stronger. All around them were clouds of swirling white. Surely, they'd be able to spot Katerina? But there was nothing. Nothing but endless drifts of snow and ice.

After a few more minutes of running, Veter slowed. But why? There was no sign of Katerina.

Zima began to ask Veter why he'd stopped when something caught her eye. A piece of blue fabric poking out of the snow, fluttering in the wind. She pointed with a shivering finger, and Mrs. Orlova expertly guided them toward the clue.

As soon as they halted, Zima descended from the sleigh and waded through the snow to get a closer look. As she approached, there was a low groan. Then a shadow moved. It was a person, curled up and huddled against a snowbank. The drift formed a wall around the shivering form.

Zima knew the truth even as they approached. The whispering forest voices had grown louder and more urgent, repeating Katerina's name over and over, overpowering the roaring wind.

Veter and Nadya hastened to join Zima. Together they knelt down to get a closer look. It was Katerina. Icicles crusted in her hair, and her eyes were closed.

A wave of despair engulfed Zima. Katerina, lost in the snow. How long had she been alone?

But they were here. It would all be okay. It wasn't too late.

Veter prodded Katerina with his nose and began to lick

her face, trying to warm her. Mrs. Orlova made her way over to them, a look of sick horror draining all color from her cheeks.

"Katerina!" Nadya shouted, cupping Katerina's face in her hands. "Katerina, wake up!"

Katerina's eyelids flicked open, but closed again, as though ice weighed them down. Her head lolled against her shoulder.

"We have to get her inside!" Mrs. Orlova shouted. But before Zima could answer, there was a groan from Katerina.

"Baba Yaga . . . ," Katerina croaked, her eyes still closed. "I'm so sorry." She took in great gasping breaths and clutched at her chest.

"It will be okay," said Zima, trying to reassure herself as much as Katerina.

Together Mrs. Orlova, Zima, and Nadya lifted Katerina and carried her to the sleigh. Mrs. Orlova took off her cloak and placed it over the young witch. Katerina's eyes opened again.

"It wasn't a curse," she said to Nadya. "It was a warning. . . ." Zima could barely hear her over the roar of the storm.

"It's okay now. We'll have you safe soon . . . ," Zima said in her most soothing voice, bending close.

Veter leapt into the sleigh and began to lick Katerina's face again. He lay beside her, pressed close so his fur could warm her.

Katerina looked at Zima. She wheezed as she tried to form the words. "The doll . . . my object . . . I didn't b-b-believe you." Katerina moaned again and dug her fingers into Veter's fur, twisting.

"What do you mean?"

"That without it . . . I would . . . fade . . ."

Her head sank back against the sleigh. Her face had gone a dangerous shade of gray. They were losing her.

CHAPTER 45

"The doll . . . ," Nadya heard Katerina whisper to Zima. "Without it . . . I would . . . fade . . ."

The doll. Nadya sifted through her memories. The warning Katerina said Baba Yaga had given her, that her life depended on her embracing her magic. Katerina giving her the doll. Katerina falling ill.

She remembered the strange, lifelike quality of the doll. And Zima's words: that a witch needed an object, something made of the forest.

Suddenly Nadya's breath caught in her throat. The doll was Katerina's object. Being without it all this time had been killing her.

And Nadya had left it at the orphanage!

Nadya hauled herself into the sleigh as Zima and Mrs. Orlova climbed up beside her.

"Mrs. Orlova, we have to get back!" Nadya shouted over the wind. "Quick!"

As Mrs. Orlova pulled the reins, Nadya held her breath. Katerina's life had been draining out of her ever since she'd given the doll to Nadya. How much time did she have left?

A lamp bobbed behind them on the road. Was it the tsar?

Mrs. Orlova urged the horse faster, but the light was still gaining on them.

Nadya moved to hide Katerina, covering her with Mrs. Orlova's cloak.

The light drew closer, and another sleigh pulled up beside them, floating like a swan on a lake. And seated inside it were Izel, Oksana, and a few maids and footmen from the castle. They were a warming vision in the middle of this frozen expanse of hills.

"We have to get out of this storm!" shouted Izel. "You need to hide. His soldiers are coming!"

One of the servants offered more blankets to wrap around Katerina, and then they set off again, racing over the hills as fast as the horses would take them.

* * *

As soon as they reached the orphanage, Izel and Mrs. Orlova worked to carry Katerina from the sleigh through the kitchen door. The others followed close behind.

Nadya picked up the doll from the floor. The crooked smile painted on its face was worn but still showed, as though the doll was trying to reassure Nadya that everything would be fine. Katerina was of the forest, just like this little doll. She cradled it close to her chest. It would help Katerina be well again. It had to.

Katerina lay on a bench that had been pulled close to the warm oven. The others watched her, twisting their hands nervously and blinking back tears. "I have it! What do I do?" Nadya called, holding out the doll.

Zima took it from her. "I'm not quite sure," she said, but she placed it next to Katerina, then arranged Katerina's arm so that her hand rested on the doll's belly.

Katerina's breathing was labored and slow, her blue lips open.

They watched in horrified silence, waiting for something to happen.

The sight made Nadya ill. She'd had the doll all along. She could have brought it with her to the castle, and Katerina would have been fine. But now Katerina was dying, and it was all Nadya's fault.

Katerina had to get better. Nadya couldn't lose her.

But as Katerina lay still, the hope that was flickering inside Nadya shuddered, as though threatening to go out. What if they hadn't retrieved the doll in time? What if they were too late? She squeezed her eyes closed. No, Katerina would be okay.

As Nadya opened her eyes again, Katerina's fingers twitched. One twirled the grass hair of the doll. Her chest rose and fell. And at last her eyelids fluttered open.

Relief flooded Nadya. It warmed her insides more than Mrs. Orlova's oven.

Little by little, color returned to Katerina's face as she held the doll. At last, she was able to ask for some water. Nadya dashed to grab a ladle for her, then let Katerina sip from it slowly. Mrs. Orlova set about burning scented herbs and brewing some tea. Veter padded close to Katerina and laid his head on her lap. Mrs. Orlova eyed him warily, but seemed to slowly accept that he wanted Katerina to be well just as they all did.

Tears glistened on Katerina's eyelashes. She touched the soft fur on Veter's ears. "Thank you. I thought . . . I thought I wouldn't wake up."

"Why were you out there in the storm?" asked Mrs. Orlova.

"I couldn't stay, not when I realized . . . the tsar lied . . . he told me he knew how to rid me of my powers." Katerina reached for Zima's hand. "You'd warned me about him, about his scheming and lies, but I didn't want to believe you." She looked back to Nadya. "But, Nadya—she said you could be trusted. I realized soon after Nadya left that I already knew the truth."

Nadya had always thought of Katerina as frustratingly perfect, yet here she was, admitting she made a mistake. Zima wasn't the real Baba Yaga, but they'd seen in the memory how much the real Baba Yaga had wanted to keep Katerina safe. The old witch had wanted to protect Katerina all along.

Katerina took the teacup Mrs. Orlova offered her and stared down at the dark liquid. "You made me see what I didn't want to see," she said to Nadya. She sighed, but her lips twitched with the hint of a smile. "I feared the forest because of its power. I tried to run away, but I couldn't."

She swirled the tea in her cup and took a sip. "I have hidden from myself, and I can't anymore. I've spent too long pretending." Fire blazed in her eyes as she said, "I am the next Baba Yaga."

Nadya heard Katerina's words with pride, feeling closer to her than ever. They both had tried to run away in the hopes of finding something. But what they'd found was each other.

CHAPTER 46

Zima and the others, human and wolf alike, listened to Katerina's story in solemn silence.

What Grom had told her about Baba Yaga was wrong, she knew that now. When she'd gone to Baba Yaga, it was a betrayal of his trust. But it was what she had to do to save Leto.

And Grom was also trying to save their pack. Veter had told Zima of Grom's plan to attack the village, and she knew Grom truly thought it was necessary.

She could feel Grom's presence deep in her stomach, solid as a tree trunk. He was a part of her, and their separation was a slow and steady ache. Before becoming Baba Yaga she'd never appreciated what it meant to have him step up as the head of their pack. How tired and frightened he must have felt, missing their parents but putting on a brave face for the others. Maybe he didn't accept Zima's help leading the pack because he didn't want her sharing in his burden.

He was doing what he thought was right. And only Zima could tell him that he was wrong.

From somewhere outside, a wolf howled.

It was answered by another. And another. The howls rang through the walls and windows. Zima felt her jaw tremble.

They were here. The moment of the attack had come. She had to stop them before anyone got hurt.

She went to the door. Snow and dry leaves flitted across the floor as she opened it. The winds had slowed. A deathly silence filled the yard, and the clouds had parted to reveal the silver glow of moonlight. She stepped over the threshold, expecting she would have to face her family alone. But a rustle behind her made her turn, and she realized that the others had stood to follow. Veter, Nadya, Katerina, Oksana . . . all of them were preparing to join her.

Another howl echoed, amplified by the houses and the chill in the air. Veter padded forward, sniffing. He led the group up the hill toward the forest, the way they'd first come. The gleam of firelight from Baba Yaga's hut was just visible through the trees.

Figures moved in the darkness. And then the wolves

emerged. Grom, Leto, even Potok, and behind them, wolves from other packs. A crowd of them. Somehow Grom had convinced them all to join him in this senseless attack.

As soon as the wolves spotted the strange group of humans, witches, and wolves, Grom trotted forward to stand in the lead. His eyes landed first on Veter, with barely disguised contempt, and then on Zima.

Baba Yaga, said Grom, *I was not expecting you.* His voice was a roll of thunder. Zima could almost feel the blood pounding through the veins of the wolves. They were eager to attack, to fight. They were itching to run and jump and bite.

"I'm not Baba Yaga," she said, yet even as she said it, she knew that in some small way, she was. "I am Zima."

Grom snorted in disbelief at first, but something made him pause. He moved toward her, the snow crunching beneath his heavy paws. It was difficult to tell if he moved in anger or relief or another emotion altogether.

He lifted his muzzle to sniff her in greeting. As a wolf, Zima was supposed to bow to him, to submit to his authority. But she would not bow to him today. After everything she'd been through, she couldn't go along with this plan of his. It was the wrong way to keep the pack safe. He had to understand that.

She stared into his eyes, and she could see him waiting for her to bow. She stood firm.

He pulled away.

What has she done to you? he asked. He wasn't angry. There was a sadness in his voice at the question. *I was sure you'd been killed.*

"It was the price to save Leto."

Where have you been? You should have come to us.

"I wanted to protect the pack. I've been living with the humans in the castle." She turned and gave a small smile to Izel and Oksana, who were watching the wolves nervously.

Grom's expression brightened. *You've been learning how to defeat them.*

There was a ripple of interest among the other wolves. They gathered closer to hear Zima's words.

"I learned of a planned hunt that threatened our pack, and went to the castle to stop it," Zima said. She could feel the excitement of the other wolves and from Grom and Leto, and see the anxiety in Potok's eyes. They were all waiting to hear what she would say.

It was the attention and respect she'd always wanted.

When they heard what she had to say next, it would all go away. She would be reviled. Some of the wolves might even try to attack her as a traitor. But she had to say it.

"We've spent so long fearing all humans and witches. Ever since the humans started coming into the forest we've grown more and more afraid." The other wolves shuffled their paws. Potok's tail and ears flicked. "But we only need to fear those humans who would do us harm. And I've found one human who wishes to harm us beyond all others," she said.

Grom's brow furrowed. *Who?*

"Tsar Aleksander. The humans coming into the forest, the great fire, it all began with him. And now he has a plan to destroy the forest itself. He's coming here, looking for me, and for Katerina." She turned to the young witch standing behind her. Katerina stepped forward, her chin high, only a twitching in her fingers showing any hint of nervousness. "We have to protect her from him." Behind her, Mrs. Orlova, Nadya, and the others murmured their agreement.

There was a low rumble in the distance. Zima turned. Along the road to the castle, a group of soldiers on horseback were moving across the landscape, slithering over the hills like a giant snake. Their armor was black against the snow, and torches blazed, blood-red against the inky sky. At the sight, the wolves stood their ground, baring their fangs and readying themselves for an attack.

It could all be over. The wolves could defeat the tsar and his men when they arrived and end the threat once and for all.

But violence led to fear. Fear led to more violence. Zima didn't want to attack the tsar; she wanted to keep him from wielding and controlling the magic of the forest.

Zima raised her voice so that all the wolves could hear. "This man is the one who wants to harm us. He'll hurt anyone who gets in his way—wolves, witches, and villagers."

The wolves were still in their attack positions, but they watched her, listening. She had their attention.

"The one thing he's afraid of," Zima said, realizing the truth of the words as she spoke them, "is the forest. It's why he wants power and control over it. If we can lure him into the forest, we can defeat him!" It seemed dangerous, foolish even, to bring the tsar to the very forest he was trying to destroy. But she knew now that magic could overpower the tsar without bloodshed, as sure as she'd done magic in the dungeons.

She waited while the wolves took in her words.

None of the wolves moved.

The tsar's soldiers galloped forward, their horses' hooves churning the snow and their swords glinting in the torchlight. At the lead rode Tsar Aleksander astride his midnight stallion. Several hills separated them, but at the pace the soldiers were galloping, they would be upon them in minutes. The humans grimaced with fear, as if they were eager to hide inside the orphanage. But they didn't move; instead, they watched Zima, waiting for her instructions.

Zima's heart pounded. If they waited much longer, the tsar's soldiers would descend before the wolves had a chance to enter the protection of the trees. They would all be caught exposed, defenseless. She couldn't let that happen.

She looked to her older brother. "Please, Grom," she said. "Sometimes protecting the pack means choosing safety over a fight. Believing that some witches and humans can be trusted. We have to work together in this. I need you to trust *me*."

Grom watched her, uncertainty in his eyes.

"If we retreat to the forest, if we trust its magic," she said, "our pack will be the safest we've ever been." The village would be safe too.

She watched the fear and confusion in his face shift to a look of determination. Finally, he stepped forward, and bowed low to Zima. He was following her lead and telling the other wolves to do the same.

They watched him, weighing their decision. She could see the choice they faced. If they attacked the soldiers in the middle of the village, there was a good chance every wolf would die in the effort. They didn't want to trust her, but doing so just might save them. Their packs, and the forest.

One by one, the other wolves around the circle bowed their heads as well. Not to Grom, but to Zima. They were putting their trust in her. They were looking to her to lead. She couldn't let them down.

Zima bowed to the wolves before her, thanking them for their trust. Together, the wolves lifted their noses and howled. The sound filled her heart to overflowing. She was going to burst. "Into the forest!" she shouted.

As one, the wolves turned and everyone moved forward into the protection of the trees.

CHAPTER 47

Baba Yaga's ears flicked in agitation. Her hut was barely sheltered by the skeletal trees at the edge of the forest.

What mischief had that wolf been up to? She'd hoped the raven would have kept things under tighter control.

But as she climbed the steps, her annoyance was replaced by the excitement of being home again. Of seeing the raven and that wolf again. Soon she would no longer be alone. Perhaps there was still some hope they could all defeat the tsar together.

She pushed the door open with her paw. Firelight and warmth surged forward, cloaking her and drawing her inside.

The hut was empty.

She twisted around. Through the door, the darkness of the night outside appeared solid, dense as packed snow.

They had abandoned her.

Her paws barely touched the steps as she raced back outside. She found a patch of bare earth, sheltered from snow by the trees, and laid down to sense the magic of the forest in the soil beneath her. But gone was the pulse that had always drummed through her whenever she stayed silent enough to listen.

No magic. No assistance. She was truly alone.

She looked around. Tree branches rustled in the freezing night air. The moon above stared down at her.

The forest and all its inhabitants were depending on her. Soon there would be nothing left to protect.

She would have to do this herself.

The wolf blood inside her grew hot. The moon called to her.

Her bones shuddered. A howl filled her throat. It leapt from her, climbing toward the sky, soaring overhead and away.

"You are more of a wolf than I realized," said a voice.

Baba Yaga opened her eyes. Ivan stood beside the hut, his smile lit by the firelight that shone through the door.

You came on your own, she said in wonder.

"It was strange," he said. "As soon as I realized I wanted to find you, a path seemed to open up before me."

Baba Yaga's lips parted in a wolfish grin. *You are most welcome in my hut.*

"It looks like I've arrived just in time," said Ivan. He gestured in the direction of the village.

Something shimmered in the distance.

From the edge of the forest, the shadowy figures of wolves and humans were moving toward them.

Perhaps she was not so alone after all.

CHAPTER 48

Howls echoed through Zima's blood. She followed the racing wolves as quickly as she could, Katerina and the others at her elbow.

Magic tingled around her as she entered the protection of the forest. Just before her was Baba Yaga's hut, its door unexpectedly open.

A familiar voice snapped, *Where have you been?*

A figure approached, and Zima found herself looking into the orange eyes of her wolf body.

"I could ask you the same question!" cried Zima.

Baba Yaga's nose twitched, but she didn't answer.

"What's going on?" asked Katerina. Her gaze flitted

between wolf and witch, as if she could sense the connection between them, but couldn't work out why it was there.

"I'm not Baba Yaga. I'm a wolf," said Zima, jabbing her cane at the witch inhabiting her wolf body. "This is Baba Yaga!"

Nadya, Izel, and the others were silent, their eyes flicking between Zima and Baba Yaga. But Katerina looked hurt. She turned to the real Baba Yaga. "You weren't the one who helped me?"

You helped her? Baba Yaga asked.

Zima nodded. "With my friends," she said, gesturing at the now-familiar faces around her.

"But where *have* you been?" asked Katerina. Spots of color had appeared in her cheeks.

I had to set things right, said Baba Yaga. *Everything, not just defeating the tsar. I needed the tsar who would be best for the village and the forest: the true tsar, Ivan.* She glanced at the young man standing beside her, who was watching Katerina with an expression of wonder and delight, like a pup seeing a falling star for the first time.

Grom stood away from the group, watching Baba Yaga with obvious distrust, his tail stiff and his ears alert. *The tsar is gathering villagers to join him and his soldiers,* he cut in. *They are coming.*

We need to protect Katerina, said Veter. *Get the hut to hide her.*

"No," said Zima, Katerina, and Baba Yaga all at once.

Katerina stepped forward. Behind her, Nadya and Mrs. Orlova watched in admiration. Before her, the wolves and Baba Yaga stood between her and the forest beyond. "It's my duty now to protect the forest, and that's what I'm going to do. I can't hide from it."

With a steadying breath to calm her shaking legs, Zima took her place beside Katerina, and together they turned to face the village. All the wolves, along with Baba Yaga and Ivan, formed a wall behind her, a barrier between the tsar and the magic he intended to steal. He wouldn't get past them.

An eerie silence fell. Torches moved toward them in the

darkness. A horde of humans from the village had joined the soldiers. At the front of the group rode Tsar Aleksander, his hulking form enlarged by his fur cloak. In the moonlight the angry lines across his forehead and at the corners of his mouth were carved in stark relief. Approaching horse hooves crunched in the snow.

"How shocking to discover you had gone, my dear beloved bride," he sneered at Katerina. "It can't be that you've changed your mind. Do you now wish to become a witch?" His eyes slid to Zima, barely hiding his disgust, before returning to Katerina. "You could join me. Together, as tsar and tsaritsa, we would be more powerful than either of us alone."

But Katerina ignored him, addressing the villagers behind him instead. "Friends, please, you don't have to follow the tsar."

The villagers murmured among themselves, weighing their fury at the tsar's threat of execution against their distrust of the forest. One of them called out, "But he said we'd be executed!" and another, "Why are you with the witch?" The villagers' voices rose, accusing Baba Yaga of bewitching Katerina. "She threatens us all!"

Katerina shook her head. "She will save us. She already saved me"—she nodded toward Tsar Aleksander—"from him."

Nadya's voice chimed in. "And she saved me."

"All this time she has been our guardian, and we've feared and hated her," Katerina said. She looked down at the real Baba Yaga, and then lifted her gaze to Zima. "We should not fear the forest, but we should respect it. It is dangerous, but it is not evil. I now know that it's an honor to be Baba Yaga, to protect the forest. And I will strive to be worthy of that responsibility."

Deep rumbling laughter shook the tsar's shoulders. He dismounted from his horse and swaggered forward to face Katerina and Zima. "Enough of this. Tell me, witch," he said, his cold eyes staring at Zima, "how can I stop you from further disrupting my plans?"

Zima's heart stopped. If the curse of truth applied to her, she could doom them all.

He waited, a confident grin gleaming in the moonlight.

But Zima said nothing. The tsar's pact with Baba Yaga did not bind her. She was not the true Baba Yaga and she felt no compulsion to answer.

His smile stiffened, and confusion twitched in the corners of his eyes. But he soon masked any discomfort. "I will give you one last chance," he said, his voice low and deadly. "Join me, and I will spare the village."

Behind him, soldiers moved to the edge of the village, holding their burning torches near the dry wood of the cottages. A wave of fear and horror coursed through the villagers. More soldiers marched toward Baba Yaga's hut, and one extended his torch to its feet. The flames lashed at its legs.

Not the hut! The hut had become almost like a friend. He had no right to burn it. A growl escaped her throat.

Gripping her cane, Zima thrust her palm forward. With a rumble like the earth itself was crying out, the soil beneath the tsar's feet gave way. Rocks tumbled down into a great cavern below.

Horses whinnied and villagers screamed. One of the soldiers' torches fell and ignited the twigs scattered across the ground between drifts of snow.

"Put it out!" Katerina shouted. Izel and Mrs. Orlova dashed forward, trying to smother the flames with their cloaks. Katerina, Oksana, and Nadya moved to help villagers from the edge of the chasm.

Zima kept her attention on the crumbling earth, focusing her energy on guiding it toward the soldiers and away from the villagers and wolves. But there was no controlling it. Soil shifted and trees tumbled. She pulled her arm back, severing the flow of magic through her. She collapsed forward, panting.

Tsar Aleksander was clinging to a ledge, legs scrambling for purchase. He grabbed a root and pulled, hoisting himself up. When he'd regained his footing, he stormed toward one of the soldiers, snatched his torch, and prepared to hurl it at Baba Yaga's hut.

But Ivan launched himself at the tsar and grabbed his arm. The tsar was a head taller than Ivan and twice as broad, but Ivan held firm. They struggled against one another. The tsar reached for his sword, but Ivan was faster. He grabbed a jeweled hilt at the tsar's hip and yanked the dagger out of its sheath.

The dagger flashed with fire and moonlight. Zima recognized its blood-red rubies and the glitter of gold. With a flick of his wrist Ivan whipped the dagger at the tsar, drawing a slash across his cheek. Blood streamed from the wound.

The tsar paid no attention to the gash. He had managed to draw his sword at last. With thundering fury he let out a roar and swung his sword in a high arc. Ivan met the tsar's sword with the dagger, and the blades pressed against one another, each man trying to force the other back.

All around them, wolves and villagers were swarming toward the soldiers. The snarls of the wolves tore through the air. Grom and Leto crouched on either side of Tsar Aleksander and Ivan, growling. The castle servants brandished kitchen knives. But the villagers and wolves were no match for the soldiers' swords.

Zima had to stop this. Now. She closed her eyes. From somewhere deep in her memory came Baba Yaga's voice, saying that magic couldn't create or destroy, it could only

alter. She grasped her cane, holding the memory in her mind, and began to chant. "Please," Zima said. "Magic of the forest . . . hear me. Defeat him. . . ."

She repeated the words over and over.

Beside her, Katerina joined in.

Power thrummed beneath her feet, but nothing was happening. The tsar was gaining an edge on Ivan, pushing him to the ground. Ivan's dagger slipped and the tsar's blade clanged against it, thrust within inches of his neck.

Baba Yaga had said that the forest listened, not just to witches. Zima looked to the wolves bravely facing the soldiers, and to the villagers. "Say the words with me!" she called to them.

Wolves and humans looked at one another nervously. No one said a word.

Then Potok began to speak. *Magic of the forest . . . defeat him*, he chanted in rhythm with Zima and Katerina.

Leto joined him.

And Nadya.

And then Oksana.

Soon the clearing was alive with the steady pulse of the magic words.

They had weapons and fire and songs and stories. But the forest had always been. The forest would always be. The forest would give them the power to defeat the tsar.

Zima watched the wolves around her, swelling with

pride. As her eyes met Grom's, he too began to chant with the others.

The air began to glow around the two witches, its light coursing toward Tsar Aleksander. It flowed and rippled like a stream. The light swelled, surrounding them.

The magic lashed at the tsar. Tendrils flicked at his ankles.

Something crawled up the tsar's legs and then down his arms to the tip of his sword. Small shoots sprouted from the sword and his wrists, growing, turning thick and wrinkled. His skin hardened. He opened his mouth to scream, but no sound emerged.

When the chanting stopped, a stately tree stood in the glade, a handful of golden leaves blowing in the breeze.

Wind swept through the clearing. The fighting stopped. Soldiers stared at the tree that was once their leader. Villagers grabbed the weapons from the soldiers' hands.

An old man among the villagers stared at Zima in fear and awe. "You did that to him?" he asked.

Katerina raised her voice. "She defeated the tsar—the village and the forest are safe!" The villagers' voices swelled into a cheer.

Zima looked out over the crowd. Wolves, villagers, and her friends from the castle, the spell could not have worked without all of them. "No," she said, holding her wrinkled hands out to the crowd, "*we* defeated the tsar!"

* * *

Zima stood silently as Izel introduced Ivan to the villagers as the long-lost heir to the tsardom. A ring he wore, with a ruby and carved eagles, seemed to prove the truth of it. Already Ivan was showing himself to be a good leader—he was listening to the villagers' concerns and comforting them. With Ivan and Katerina, Zima was sure that a peace between the forest, the village, and the castle was within reach.

Songs filled the clearing as the villagers celebrated. They danced and played. Even some of the wolves joined in, prancing and wagging their tails. Those that didn't, like Grom, watched the merriment with quiet elation shimmering in their eyes.

The wolf Baba Yaga trotted toward Zima. *Come, walk with me,* said the witch.

"Wait!" called Nadya, chasing after them, followed close behind by Oksana. Nadya wrapped her arms around Zima's middle, hugging her. "I know you say you're not really Baba Yaga, but you will always be Baba Yaga to me. Even when you're a wolf again." She pressed her face into Zima's belly. Her voice was muffled and teary as she said, "You saved us all."

Zima opened her mouth to reply, but the words caught in her throat. As a witch, she'd been able to speak to both humans and wolves. But once she became a wolf again, that power would be gone. Her wolf ears wouldn't be able to make out anything said to her by her new friends.

Zima looked to Nadya and Oksana and tried to imagine a friendship where they could no longer speak to one another.

She knelt down, and without a word, wrapped her arms around Nadya again, hoping the hug would convey the feelings thrumming inside her. They might still visit one another as human and wolf, but it would never be the same.

She stood and wiped a tear from Oksana's cheek. There

were ways to speak without words, and those would have to do.

At last, they parted, and Baba Yaga led Zima toward the edge of the forest. Pale light climbed the sky from the horizon, turning the world the deep blue of predawn. They were just in time to make the switch.

You did so much more than I ever expected, said Baba Yaga, taking a seat and curling her tail around her paws. *I am grateful to you.*

"And you think this new tsar will make everything better?" asked Zima.

Baba Yaga nodded. Her tail flicked. *I trust the forest. It knew I needed you. Not just to break the spell, but to bring us together.* The lightening sky made the silver-gray of Baba Yaga's fur shimmer as she looked at Zima. It was strange, Zima realized, looking at herself, seeing what others saw. How the outside could both reflect and hide the person within. *You can become a wolf again now. I've seen the magic you can wield.* She moved to face Zima, her paws in line with the tips of Zima's boots. *Cast the spell whenever you wish,* said the witch.

Zima swallowed. She had grown used to her strange life as a witch: having hands that could grip things, enjoying human food and songs, the ability to perform magic.

But she couldn't stay a witch forever. Sooner or later, she

had to face that reality. She was a wolf, and she needed to be in her old body again.

She wouldn't be the same wolf, though. Somehow over this past week she'd joined a world beyond her wolf pack. Wolves and humans, she sat midway between them, belonging to both and also neither. Once she became a wolf again, that door would be closed. That part of her life would be over.

She looked down at Baba Yaga. "Are you ready?" Zima asked.

Baba Yaga nodded. *Are you?*

In answer, Zima clutched the cane with both hands and closed her eyes. The wood hummed beneath her fingers. Her lips tight, she murmured, "Please . . . make me a wolf again. . . ."

A tingling began in her toes and crawled up her legs. It reached her back and shoved her forward, down onto all fours. The cane fell to the ground, sinking into the snow with a soft thud. A shiver crawled up her neck to the tip of her nose. And then it was gone. The chatter of human voices rang in her ears. When she opened her eyes, she was lower to the ground, her vision clearer. Zima lifted her hands . . . no, her paws, admiring her old claws. Twisting to look behind her, she saw her tail wagging violently.

Joy burst inside her, spreading into every limb like a stream finding its way through the forest, filling nooks and crannies and flowing onward. She lifted her head and let out a howl.

The true witch Baba Yaga stood before her. The purple in her eyes glittered, like the last stars in a sunrise. She lifted her cane from the snow and leaned upon it. "It feels good to be my old self again," she said.

Zima wondered if she would ever be *her* old self.

But now she was something different. Someone new.

And she liked that wolf better.

CHAPTER 49

aba Yaga entered the clearing, the fresh moss on the ground dampening her footsteps. The others didn't notice her approach. Zima lay with her eyes closed, her tail wagging as Nadya stroked her ears. Behind them Potok and Veter playfully fought over a stick. Only Katerina looked less than relaxed.

The voices of the forest were singing this evening, a song of mourning and celebration. Soon Baba Yaga would join them.

The setting sun spilled an orange glow over the trees and the budding crocuses. It was almost time.

Baba Yaga had known this day was approaching ever since Katerina had made a new magical object to replace her doll: a carved wooden pendant, which she wore around her neck on a chain. She wasn't a child anymore. She could protect the forest on her own.

The breeze blew Baba Yaga's hair into her eyes, strands now so white they were almost see-through. She brushed them away and couldn't help but notice that her skin had the same translucent sheen. She had taken care with her appearance. A crown of leaves, made by Nadya, was placed upon her head, and around her neck was a garland of flowers.

She stood in silence a moment longer, watching this unlikely family. Katerina noticed her first, opening her mouth to say something but struggling to find the words.

Instead, Baba Yaga spoke first. "It is time," she said.

The others flinched at the sudden sound of her voice, jarred from their contentment by what they knew was coming. They looked to each other, afraid to move. Baba Yaga smiled. She knew what they were thinking. It was too soon. It was only five moons since the defeat of the tsar, barely enough time to enjoy each other's company.

But Katerina would do well, whatever path she chose. She was as caring toward the forest and its creatures as she was toward Nadya. Her experience with the tsar had made her thoughtful, but not distrusting. Perhaps one day Katerina would even decide to marry after all. Ivan certainly seemed interested. He'd been to visit Katerina frequently after getting his family settled at their new home in the castle. Baba Yaga trusted that Katerina would make the right decision. And that meant it was time for Baba Yaga to leave.

She looked around at them all, and her eyebrow twitched. "Oh, come now, we knew this day would arrive. If you don't follow me, I'll have to go on my own," she said.

Slowly they all climbed to their feet, sorrow weighing heavily on their shoulders. As they rose, Zima's other brothers Grom and Leto arrived in the clearing. Baba Yaga was pleased to see them. Though they hadn't fully warmed to the humans, and probably would never trust them completely, they understood that Zima couldn't live the life they'd led before. She lived separately from them now, along with Veter and the nervous young Potok. But Grom and Leto clearly loved her and respected her choice, and now they were here to support Zima, knowing how difficult she would find this day.

In a line Katerina, Nadya, and the wolves followed Baba Yaga as she led the way to the stream. It had formed as the snow began to melt in the spring thaw, and much like how magic coursed through Baba Yaga, it flowed through the forest, forging its own path. The raven hovered above her, ever watchful.

Baba Yaga turned around to face them all.

"After three hundred years of living alone," she said, "I never thought I would have such a somber group beside me on this day." She held her hand out to Katerina. The young witch took it and squeezed the old woman's fingers. Baba Yaga chuckled. "Not too hard now—I am *very* old."

Katerina smiled, but her eyes sparkled with tears. The raven opened his mouth as if he wanted to say something pert, but couldn't find his voice. Instead, he landed and gave her a formal bow.

Baba Yaga looked among them, and her gaze fell on Zima as she said her final words. "I am the forest. It flows through me. And now, I will flow through it. And in this way, I'll always be here, surrounding you, a part of you."

With those words she turned and stepped into the

stream. Its steady flow was soothing. The cool water only came up to her ankles, but her skirts swirled in the current.

Baba Yaga took a deep breath, inhaling through her nose.

"I smell . . . springtime," she said.

The waters rose, and little by little, they began to carry her away, wearing her down as though she were made of nothing more than earth.

With a final contented sigh, the waters took the last of her, and she flowed away from the others, through the forest, one with the forest.

CHAPTER 50

*Z*ima moved slowly, as though dragging her paws through water. When she paused to look back at the stream where she'd last seen Baba Yaga, Veter stopped and stood beside her.

She is still here, said Veter. *In the trees, and*—he turned to Zima with bright eyes—*in you.*

Zima bowed her head. *I feel like I barely got the chance to know her.*

We are lucky for the time we get to spend with others, said Veter. *I know that now more than ever.*

I am glad you are with us, Veter, said Zima. It was hard to feel sad whenever he was around. *With me.*

Me too, he replied.

As the group gathered in the clearing, Katerina took Nadya's hand, preparing to walk her back to the orphanage, where Nadya was helping Mrs. Orlova with the younger girls. But Nadya shook her head. She said something to Katerina. Zima couldn't understand the human words. But the ache of not being able to understand was getting a little less with each passing day, even though it would always be there.

"All right, I'll sing you a song," Katerina said. With Baba Yaga gone, she was the only one who could talk to both animals and humans. She took a seat among the roots of an old tree. "After that I'll walk you home."

Zima looked to Grom. He wasn't usually one for songs. He'd told Zima that he could never bring himself to behave like a human pet. But he met her gaze. On this day of all days, the valley between them had narrowed a little. Sometimes it was wider and sometimes narrower, and Zima had learned to be grateful for the days when she and her brother could lie next to each other as they once had when they were pups, close enough to feel each other's heartbeat. She wouldn't trade the changes for anything, but she was glad for the chance to remember old times too.

Grom approached and lay down next to her. Veter joined her on the other side. Their closeness eased the ache in her heart. But Baba Yaga would still be there, part of the forest. Perhaps she would even listen to the song Katerina was about to begin.

Katerina reached up to her shoulder as if she expected to pet the raven, but he was gone. Where was he? Zima sniffed, trying to catch his scent. He'd been there only a moment ago. But before she could stand up to look for him, he reappeared, towing a branch in his claws. The tart scent reached Zima's nose, and her mouth watered. Blackberries!

He hopped toward Zima, squawking. It made Zima laugh a little. She wasn't sure she missed being able to understand his sarcastic quips. He broke off a cluster with his beak and placed it in front of Zima. She slurped up a berry, enjoying the tangy juice as the tiny fruits burst on her tongue.

"There, now," said Katerina, smiling, and she began to sing. Her voice combined the sweetness of birdcalls with the words of a human, and she sang of a young witch greeting the trees, the stars, the critters and creatures in the forest.

Zima glanced around the circle at the family she was born into, and the family she'd found. Tonight they were together, both sides of her at once. Her heart swelled with pride and love. This was her pack. And she was home.

AUTHOR'S NOTE

Baba Yaga, Ivan Tsarevich, the firebird, and the gray wolf all appear in at least one Russian fairy tale. Baba Yaga and Ivan each appear in many.

One of those stories that heavily inspired this one is "Tsarevich Ivan, the Firebird, and the Gray Wolf," where a wolf saves Ivan's life and wins him the tsardom. But Ivan is different in every story. His name is treated like a place-holder that belongs to any hero—prince or peasant. Ivan could be anyone, which is why he has one of the most common names in Russia.

Baba Yaga is also different from story to story, though unlike Ivan, she always felt to me like the same Baba Yaga. She has so many delightful details about her across dozens of tales, many of which I tried to include in different drafts of this book but ended up deleting because they were distracting or confusing. I especially love her servants, who ride through the forest on a red horse, a white horse, and a black horse to bring about the dawn, day, and night to the forest. Her hut is often described as "spinning on its legs" and surrounded by a fence of bones. She can also be three sisters, all named Baba Yaga. Sometimes she will give the heroes tools to help them on their journey; sometimes she's a villain to be thwarted. It was this aspect of her character that became a seedling for *A Wolf for a Spell*.

We're used to the "Big Bad Wolf" in Western folklore. But the gray wolf helps Ivan Tsarevich win everything he desires, similar to the fairy godmother in Cinderella. Like Baba Yaga, wolves can be good or bad.

These stories of the Big Bad Wolf and our fear of wolves over many centuries have led to many of the world's wolf populations being hunted to near extinction. Different countries now have environmental movements to protect wolf populations. Wolves are wild, but they are also loving, beautiful, and intelligent. It's my hope that with this story, you question the fears we have of witches and wolves, and fight for the wolves' homes, just as Zima would.

ACKNOWLEDGMENTS

There was a point when writing this book where I couldn't figure out how all the pieces fit together. My partner and husband, Ralph, asked me to tell him the story out loud. We used props to signify the different characters, with avocados serving as the humans, and potatoes as the witches. Wolves were citrus: Zima and Grom were played by oranges, and the younger wolves were lemons. I moved them around on the tabletop, like pieces on a chessboard, and told the story. The humor of this situation and Ralph's keen story-telling insight helped us work out together what needed to happen. Ralph, thank you for supporting me through such an intense journey this past decade, for making me laugh, making dinners, and reminding me to go for walks.

I am lucky enough to have two Katerinas who made this book a reality. Thank you to Katie Grimm, my incredible agent, who showed me a vision for this book that I never dared hope it could be. Your sense of humor and inspiring brainstorming sessions make me so glad to be on your team. And thank you to Katherine Harrison, my brilliant editor, who went completely above and beyond what I ever would have imagined from an editor, offering sharp structural and sentence-level feedback but also packaging this book into something I am immensely grateful for and proud of.

Pauliina (better known online as Pauhami): I fell in love with your gorgeous illustrations from the moment Katherine sent me your Instagram handle. I tried to tell myself not to be heartbroken if you said no, and I am forever delighted you said yes. Thank you for creating illustrations so perfect and timeless, and thank you to Bob Bianchini for your incredible design. You've made something truly breathtaking.

Thank you to Jake Eldred, Artie Bennett, Marianne Cohen, Iris Broudy, Gianna Lakenauth, and everyone at Knopf Books for Young Readers and Random House Children's Books who put so much work into this book. I am an author you never met on an island on the other side of the world, and you welcomed me into your family.

K. C. Held, my Pitch Wars mentor in 2017, granted me the first opportunity to show this book to the world, and saved it from being a complete disaster in 2016 with feedback she was in no way obligated to give. None of the rest of this would have happened without you. And to fellow PW17 mentees who read this book and offered so much support, including Diana, Scott, Arianne, Adrianna, Jennifer, Rajani, and Remy: thank you.

Jenia Yudytska is a gem. I was hoping for your feedback on the depiction of Russian culture, and you gave me so much more, including historical context and new ideas, and steering me away from bad ones. Anything that's still wrong is probably something you pointed out to me and I ignored for silly plot reasons. Спасибо.

Polly read some of the earliest drafts of this book, listened to countless sessions of me agonizing over how to make it work while we ate gelato, and even speed-read it before I sent it to agents. Thank you for laughing at all my terrible notes to myself. This book would have been a mess without you.

Donna Muñoz, thank you for being my first champion, and for pushing me to enter Pitch Wars. The world needs your stories.

Iain McCaig . . . I admire you to the moon and back. Thank you for talking plot structure to me while I was in Disney World. Thank you for your valuable time, and for gushing over how great Baba Yaga is. You made this book so much better.

To other friends who supported this endeavor with their

encouragement, homes, cups of tea, who reminded me to take care of myself, and who celebrated every win—Kathy, Claire, Lauren, Sarah, Graci, Miqdad, the MGicalMisfits, the Welly Wonkadoodles, KidLit 411, Sub It Club, KidLit Alliance, and Roaring 20s group—thank you forever.

I saved my family for last, even though they were first. My mom, to whom this book is dedicated, encouraged me from a young age to be proud of our Russian and Polish background and to feel joy and pride in the culture. This book is my love letter and thank-you to you for everything. I hope Grandpa and Grandma would have liked it. And to Dad, Sabrina, Maia, and Matt, thank you for being a loving and supportive family, who have always encouraged me in whatever new dream I decided to chase, whether it was moving across the world or writing this book. I love you.